David Herbert Lawrence w... ... in 1885, fourth of the five chil... ... He attended Nottingham High ... ... His first novel, *The White ...* ... weeks after the death of his ... he had been abnormally close. At this time he finally ended his relationship with Jessie Chambers (the Miriam of *Sons and Lovers*) and became engaged to Louie Burrows. His career as a schoolteacher was ended in 1911 by the illness which was ultimately diagnosed as tuberculosis.

In 1912 Lawrence eloped to Germany with Frieda Weekley, the German wife of his former modern languages tutor. They were married on their return to England in 1914. Lawrence was now living, precariously, by his writing. His greatest novels, *The Rainbow* and *Women in Love*, were completed in 1915 and 1919. The former was suppressed, and he could not find a publisher for the latter.

After the war Lawrence began his 'savage pilgrimage' in search of a more fulfilling mode of life than industrial Western civilization could offer. This took him to Sicily, Ceylon, Australia and, finally, New Mexico. The Lawrences returned to Europe in 1925. Lawrence's last novel, *Lady Chatterley's Lover*, was banned in 1928, and his paintings confiscated in 1929. He died in Vence in 1930 at the age of 44.

Lawrence spent most of his short life living. Nevertheless he produced an amazing quantity of work – novels, stories, poems, plays, essays, travel books, translations and letters ... After his death Frieda wrote: 'What he had seen and felt and known he gave in his writing to his fellow men, the splendour of living, the hope of more and more life ... a heroic and immeasurable gift.'

Keith Sagar is Reader in English Literature in the Extra-Mural Department of the University of Manchester. Dr Sagar is the author of *The Art of D. H. Lawrence* (1966), *The Art of Ted Hughes* (1975 and 1978), *D. H. Lawrence – a Calendar of His Works* (1979), *The Life of D. H. Lawrence* (1980), *The Reef and Other Poems* (1980) and *D. H. Lawrence: Life into Art* (Penguin 1985). He has also edited several books, including two of the Lawrence volumes in Penguin, *Sons and Lovers* and (with his wife, Melissa Partridge) *The Complete Short Novels*. He is now editing volume seven of Lawrence's letters for the Cambridge edition, and working on a *magnum opus*, *Worshippers of Nature*.

D. H. LAWRENCE

POEMS

SELECTED AND INTRODUCED
BY KEITH SAGAR

REVISED EDITION

PENGUIN BOOKS

PENGUIN BOOKS

Published by the Penguin Group
27 Wrights Lane, London W8 5TZ, England
Viking Penguin Inc., 40 West 23rd Street, New York, New York 10010, USA
Penguin Books Australia Ltd, Ringwood, Victoria, Australia
Penguin Books Canada Ltd, 2801 John Street, Markham, Ontario, Canada L3R 1B4
Penguin Books (NZ) Ltd, 182–190 Wairau Road, Auckland 10, New Zealand

Penguin Books Ltd, Registered Offices: Harmondsworth, Middlesex, England

First published as *Selected Poems* in Penguin Books 1972
Reprinted with minor revisions 1975
Revised edition 1986
3 5 7 9 10 8 6

Printed and bound in Great Britain by
Cox & Wyman Ltd, Reading
Filmset in Sabon by
Rowland Phototypesetting Ltd
Bury St Edmunds, Suffolk

Contents

· 1912–18 ·
from *'Look! We Have Come Through!'*

from *Bay*

· 1920–23 ·
from *Birds, Beasts and Flowers*

from *Nettles* and *More Pansies*

from *Last Poems*

INTRODUCTION

THE very scope of Lawrence's achievement in so many other forms – fiction, travel-writing, essays, criticism, letters, and plays – has told against his standing as a poet. We have come to think of his poetry as something of a by-product of, or relaxation from, other more strenuous and important work. Though it certainly came more easily than his fiction, I am sure that, except perhaps in *Pansies*, Lawrence did not think of his poetry in this way. At the outset of his career he devoted much time and care to his poems and cherished them when written. And at three subsequent periods of his life his poetry became the primary channel of his experience and creative energy: the first year of his relationship with Frieda (*'Look! We Have Come Through!'*), the two years in Sicily (*Birds, Beasts and Flowers*), and the last year of his life (*More Pansies* and *Last Poems*).

Lawrence wrote nearly 1,000 poems, and we must concede that an unusually high proportion are unsuccessful. He needs to be read in selection. Reviewing Lawrence's *Complete Poems*, D. J. Enright wrote:

> It must be granted that this *Complete Poems* – however grateful many of us will be to have it – makes for oppressive, confusing and blunted reading. There is still room for a critical selection; none of those I have seen conveys a true sense of the fantastic variety and scope of Lawrence's verse.

I have tried to fill this gap. Moreover, I have tried to bring together in one volume all Lawrence's really successful, achieved poems – the poems on which his claim to the status of a major poet must rest.

I believe that on the strength of these 150 poems we can support the claim that Lawrence is a great poet in every sense, including the technical. The technique for making something out of nothing he had not, nor the technique of highly finished formal craftsmanship. Such technique might have improved some of his early poems. It might equally have prevented him going on to write the great poems, where the form is the perfect incarnation of the content, the perfect vehicle for the liveliness of thought and feeling, the freshness and depth of perception, the wit and wisdom he has to offer.

Many of the early poems printed here are in versions different from those with which the reader may be familiar. Lawrence extensively revised, and in some cases rewrote, these poems when preparing his *Collected Poems* in 1928. In his introductory note to that edition Lawrence says that he has tried to establish a chronological order,

because many of the poems are so personal that, in their fragmentary fashion, they make up a biography of an emotional and inner life.

Yet he goes on to say that some are

a good deal rewritten. They were struggling to say something which it takes a man twenty years to be able to say . . . A young man is afraid of his demon and puts his hand over the demon's mouth sometimes and speaks for him. And the things the young man says are very rarely poetry. So I have tried to let the demon say his say, and to remove the passages where the young man intruded.

The result, even when the poems are improved, which is not always, is a kind of ventriloquism, with the voice of the mature Lawrence speaking, sometimes grotesquely, through the mouth of the dumb young man. How ridiculous, for example, to suppose that the young man of twenty-two, out of his actual virginity, could have written the version of 'Virgin Youth' which appears in the *Collected Poems*. It is a poem by the author of *Lady Chatterley's Lover*. It seems to me much more important that we should have what the young man actually wrote at twenty-two than what Lawrence at forty-two (a much better poet, but a different man with a different demon) thought he should have written. I have therefore taken the texts from *Love Poems*, *Amores*, *New Poems* and *Bay* where they first appeared in book form.

The earliest poems date from the period 1906–8 when Lawrence was a student at Nottingham University College. The girl who figures in many of them is his first sweetheart, Jessie Chambers, the Miriam of *Sons and Lovers*. The rest of the early poems were written between 1908 and 1911, when Lawrence was teaching in Croydon. The best of them are distinguished by what Alfred Alvarez has called Lawrence's 'emotional realism'. Candour, truth and power of feeling often burst through the conventional frame in startling imagery: the voices of the parents in his childhood remembered as slender and thick lashes competing with the terrible whips of the ash-tree outside, shrieking in a storm at night; cherries hanging round the ears of a girl seen as blood-drops, thus linking her offer of love with the dead birds under the cherry tree; sex and violence again linked by potent imagery in 'Renascence', 'Snap-Dragon' and 'Cruelty and Love'; striking images of light and dark, colour and movement; images which presage the mature Lawrence – rainbows, dolphins, the long sea journey through 'the grandeur of night' to the amazing newness of dawn, resurrection, and the return to Paradise.

In 1913 Lawrence wrote to Edward Marsh:

I have always tried to get an emotion out in its own course, without altering it. It needs the finest instinct imaginable, much finer than the skill of the craftsmen . . . I don't write for your ear . . . I can't tell you what *pattern* I see in any poetry, save one complete thing.

But Lawrence's instinct, at this stage of his career, worked fitfully, and there was little craftsmanship to fall back on. He had no ear for formal rhythm or rhyme, and when he attempted them was usually inept.

Occasionally, in these early poems, the rhythm briefly frees itself and springs to life:

Rabbits, handfuls of brown earth, lie
Low-rounded on the mournful grass they have bitten down to the
      quick.
Are they asleep? – Are they alive? – Now see, when I
Move my arms the hill bursts and heaves under their spurting kick.

Sometimes he achieves the moving colloquial directness and simplicity of Brecht:

> But when I meet the weary eyes
> The reddened aching eyes of the bar-man with thin arms,
> I am glad to go back where I came from.

Particularly impressive are the four dialect poems, on the strength of which Pound proposed Lawrence for the Polignac Prize. Here Lawrence is able to forget Swinburne, Meredith and the Pre-Raphaelites and take his rhythms from the local speech he knew so well.

Lawrence never shied from sentiment for fear of sentimentality. He had the courage of his emotions, whether grief for the dead mother, sexual frustration, nostalgia for childhood, or delight in the baby which ran across the lawn to him. He expressed them all with rare delicacy. But they were the emotions of a man who had not found himself and who was at odds with his life.

Lawrence came to maturity as a poet at the same time that he came to maturity as a man and a novelist, at the time of his marriage. It is as though the new life which he launched with Frieda in 1912 and his departure from England freed him from the pressures which had retarded his development and the conventions which had crippled so much of his verse. *'Look! We Have Come Through!'* is a record of his early years with Frieda, up to the war. It is also an epithalamium, a celebration of love and marriage, not omitting the conflict and occasional misery. Marriage, Lawrence claimed, 'sort of keeps me in direct communication with the unknown, in which otherwise I am a bit lost'. His vision becomes increasingly sacramental. He does not distinguish between the creativeness which brings him and Frieda through to 'some condition of blessedness', and the creativeness which issues in poetry; neither is an achievement of the deliberate self, both are products of the wind that blows through him to which he must open and attune himself:

> Oh, for the wonder that bubbles into my soul
> I would be a good fountain, a good well-head,
> Would blur no whisper, spoil no expression.

The success of his marriage is achieved by breaking through old dead ideas and life-modes. In his art, too, he seeks to break down all the 'artificial conduits and canals through which we do so love to force our utterance', to allow the spontaneous, uniquely appropriate form to emerge. This technique produces, when successful (as it is increasingly to be), 'the perfect utterance of a concentrated spontaneous soul'. It is a far deeper and more demanding discipline than the discipline of the craftsman. Lawrence has no use for the word 'aesthetic'. The discipline is spiritual and emotional as well as linguistic. The poems are a by-product of 'that piece of supreme art, a man's life'. Some of the poems in *Look!* are personal in the restricting sense. But it is only through the wholeness and depth of personal experience that Lawrence is to create the impersonally authentic forms and universal meanings of *Birds, Beasts and Flowers*.

The horrors of the war, the moral debacle at home, the suppression of his splendid novel, *The Rainbow*, persecution, ill-health and poverty, all combined to destroy in Lawrence, during the war, his faith in humanity and a human future. He turned, to retain his sanity and faith in life, to the non-human world of birds, beasts and flowers.

Lawrence had an almost occult penetration into the being of other creatures. But in several of the best poems, the purpose is to reveal the sheer unknowable otherness of the non-human life and its strange gods. He goes to the very pale of his being, of human consciousness, and looks outward. Creatures, 'little living myths', bring him messages not only from out of the surrounding darkness, but also from the unknown depths of his own being:

In the very darkest continent of the body there is God. And from Him issue the first dark rays of our feeling, wordless, and utterly previous to words: the innermost rays, the first messengers, the primeval, honourable beasts of our being, whose voice echoes wordless and forever wordless down the darkest avenues of the soul, but full of potent speech. Our own inner meaning.

Lawrence is here making his own raid on the inarticulate. And the messengers he comes nearest to understanding are the snake and the tortoise. *Tortoises* is one long poem in six sections, a metaphysical poem about the tragedy of man's sexuality, with all the suffering, dependence, exposure that implies, and yet, ultimately, the joy, for it is a means, like death, to marriage with the universe.

There is no longer, in *Birds, Beasts and Flowers*, any sign of formal difficulty. Lawrence's demon, his daring visionary insight, speaks out clear and bold (though somewhat stridently in the less successful poems). Ostensibly about creatures, these poems explore a vast range of experience. They are dramatic confrontations between the human and non-human and potent evocations of the spirit of place. They are brimming with vitality and awareness, humour and wisdom.

Lawrence called his next volume *Pansies* because the poems are little thoughts like Pascal's *Pensées*, and because he wanted them to be thought of as unpretentious flowers blooming briefly, rather jauntily, not as monuments for posterity. He called them 'rag poems'. In the best of them we hear what Richard Hoggart has called 'the voice of a down-to-earth, tight, bright, witty Midlander . . . slangy, quick, flat and direct, lively, laconic, sceptical, non-conforming, nicely bloody-minded'. The less successful are merely 'sketches for poems', or, like the pieces of soft fruit Ibsen gave his pet scorpion, something into which Lawrence could discharge his accumulated venom.

In *More Pansies* and *Last Poems* Lawrence's thoughts become poems much more consistently than in *Pansies*. Thought is 'a man in his wholeness wholly attending' and here the poet strives to make 'a new act of attention' and then give 'direct utterance from the instant, whole man' in language that will make us prick our innermost ear. His primary theme is life's tremendous characterization and man's capacity for wonder. Now, on the brink of death, he gives us the naïve opening of a soul to life. Despite his awareness of the desperate ills of our civilization and of his own impending death, he is no longer, as he often was in *Pansies*, flippant or exasperated or spiteful. His new-found insouciance brings assurance, playfulness, and a new joy in life, in 'the magnificent here and now of life in the

16

flesh'. It is a kind of resurrection as the dying tree puts out new strange blossoms.

The clarity and splendour of these poems testify to the depth of vision they spring from – what Coleridge meant when he spoke of Wordsworth's 'sentiments':

No frequency of perusal can deprive them of their freshness. For though they are brought into the full daylight of every reader's comprehension; yet are they drawn up from depths which few in any age are privileged to visit, into which few in any age have courage to descend.

This courage manifests itself supremely in 'Bavarian Gentians' and the other poems about death. They are poignant, but never waver in their faith that death is only a part of life, the longest journey, perhaps the greatest adventure.

Keith Sagar's *D. H. Lawrence: Life into Art* (Penguin 1985) contains a full analysis of many of these poems. He has also recorded 40 of them on two cassettes which can be obtained from Audio Tapes, 740 Holloway Road, London N19 (01 281 2393/5).

Note to the Revised Edition

In the fifteen years since I prepared the original selection, I have come to realize that I underestimated Lawrence as a poet, that he wrote far more than 150 'really successful, achieved poems'; more, in fact, than can be accommodated in a selection of this size and price. However, by dropping several indifferent poems, and several long poems of rather specialized interest, I have made room for forty-five new poems. I have also rearranged the poems in a more accurately chronological order.

In 1918, in the essay 'The Spirit of Place', Lawrence formulated the law that 'every great locality expresses itself perfectly, in its own flowers, its own birds and beasts, lastly its own men, with their perfected works'. By approaching the creatures of *Birds, Beasts and Flowers* as expressions of the spirit of place, and by recognizing the myths which form the bedrock of these poems, I have come to a better understanding of the collection, which demands the inclusion of several additional poems. In three of these, 'Tropic', 'Peace' and 'Southern Night', Lawrence records how the spirit of Sicily changed him body and soul, thus making possible both the form and the content of the poems which followed, to which they form a kind of overture.

I also believe that I now understand better the imaginative thinking exemplified by many of the *Pansies*, an ability to 'fuse mind and wit with all the senses' ('Sense of Truth'). I find myself more appreciative of the satirical *Pansies*, which seem just as fresh after half a century; and the *Nettles* have lost none of their sting. Lawrence's comic gifts are still largely unrecognized.

I can guarantee that any reader who enjoys this selection will find many other poems equally to his taste in the *Complete Poems*.

KEITH SAGAR
Manchester 1985

1906–11

THE WILD COMMON

THE quick sparks on the gorse bushes are leaping,
Little jets of sunlight-texture imitating flame;
Above them, exultant, the peewits are sweeping:
They are lords of the desolate wastes of sadness their
    screamings proclaim.

Rabbits, handfuls of brown earth, lie
Low-rounded on the mournful grass they have bitten down to
    the quick.
Are they asleep? – Are they alive? – Now see, when I
Move my arms the hill bursts and heaves under their spurting
    kick.

The common flaunts bravely; but below, from the rushes
Crowds of glittering king-cups surge to challenge the
    blossoming bushes;
There the lazy streamlet pushes
Its curious course mildly; here it wakes again, leaps, laughs,
    and gushes

Into a deep pond, an old sheep-dip,
Dark, overgrown with willows, cool, with the brook ebbing
    through so slow;
Naked on the steep, soft lip
Of the bank I stand watching my own white shadow quivering
    to and fro.

What if the gorse flowers shrivelled and kissing were lost?
Without the pulsing waters, where were the marigolds and the
    songs of the brook?
If my veins and my breasts with love embossed
Withered, my insolent soul would be gone like flowers that the
    hot wind took.

So my soul like a passionate woman turns,
Filled with remorseful terror to the man she scorned, and her
    love
For myself in my own eyes' laughter burns,
Runs ecstatic over the pliant folds rippling down to my belly
    from the breast-lights above.

Over my sunlit skin the warm, clinging air,
Rich with the songs of seven larks singing at once, goes kissing
    me glad.
And the soul of the wind and my blood compare
Their wandering happiness, and the wind, wasted in liberty,
    drifts on and is sad.

Oh but the water loves me and folds me,
Plays with me, sways me, lifts me and sinks me as though it
    were living blood,
Blood of a heaving woman who holds me,
Owning my supple body a rare glad thing, supremely good.

DISCORD IN CHILDHOOD

OUTSIDE the house an ash-tree hung its terrible whips,
And at night when the wind arose, the lash of the tree
Shrieked and slashed the wind, as a ship's
Weird rigging in a storm shrieks hideously.

Within the house two voices arose in anger, a slender lash
Whistling delirious rage, and the dreadful sound
Of a thick lash booming and bruising, until it drowned
The other voice in a silence of blood, 'neath the noise of the
    ash.

DOG-TIRED

IF she would come to me here,
        Now the sunken swaths
        Are glittering paths
To the sun, and the swallows cut clear
Into the low sun – if she came to me here!

If she would come to me now,
Before the last mown harebells are dead,
While that vetch clump yet burns red;
Before all the bats have dropped from the bough
Into the cool of night – if she came to me now!

The horses are untackled, the chattering machine
Is still at last. If she would come,
I would gather up the warm hay from
The hill-brow, and lie in her lap till the green
Sky ceased to quiver, and lost its tired sheen.

I should like to drop
On the hay, with my head on her knee
And lie stone still, while she
Breathed quiet above me – we could stop
Till the stars came out to see.

I should like to lie still
As if I was dead – but feeling
Her hand go stealing
Over my face and my hair until
This ache was shed.

CHERRY ROBBERS

UNDER the long, dark boughs, like jewels red
    In the hair of an Eastern girl
Shine strings of crimson cherries, as if had bled
    Blood-drops beneath each curl.

Under the glistening cherries, with folded wings
    Three dead birds lie:
Pale-breasted throstles and a blackbird, robberlings
    Stained with red dye.

Under the haystack a girl stands laughing at me,
    With cherries hung round her ears –
Offering me her scarlet fruit: I will see
    If she has any tears.

RENASCENCE

WE have bit no forbidden apple,
    Eve and I,
Yet the splashes of day and night
Falling round us no longer dapple
The same Eden with purple and white.

This is our own still valley
    Our Eden, our home,
But day shows it vivid with feeling
And the pallor of night does not tally
With dark sleep that once covered its ceiling.

My little red heifer, to-night I looked in her eyes,
    – She will calve to-morrow:

Last night when I went with the lantern, the sow was grabbing
    her litter

With red, snarling jaws: and I heard the cries
Of the new-born, and after that, the old owl, then the bats that
    flitter.

And I woke to the sound of the wood-pigeons, and lay and
    listened,
        Till I could borrow
A few quick beats of a wood-pigeon's heart, and when I did
    rise
The morning sun on the shaken iris glistened,
And I saw that home, this valley, was wider than Paradise.

I learned it all from my Eve
        This warm, dumb wisdom.
She's a finer instructress than years;
She has taught my heart-strings to weave
Through the web of all laughter and tears.

And now I see the valley
        Fleshed all like me
With feelings that change and quiver:
And all things seem to tally
        With something in me,
Something of which she's the giver.

CRUELTY AND LOVE

WHAT large, dark hands are those at the window
Lifted, grasping the golden light
Which weaves its way through the creeper leaves
    To my heart's delight?

Ah, only the leaves! But in the west,
In the west I see a redness come
Over the evening's burning breast —
    — 'Tis the wound of love goes home!

The woodbine creeps abroad
Calling low to her lover:
   The sun-lit flirt who all the day
   Has poised above her lips in play
   And stolen kisses, shallow and gay
   Of pollen, now has gone away
   — She woos the moth with her sweet, low word,
And when above her his broad wings hover
Then her bright breast she will uncover
And yield her honey-drop to her lover.

Into the yellow, evening glow
Saunters a man from the farm below,
Leans, and looks in at the low-built shed
Where hangs the swallow's marriage bed.
   The bird lies warm against the wall.
   She glances quick her startled eyes
   Towards him, then she turns away
   Her small head, making warm display
   Of red upon the throat. His terrors sway
   Her out of the nest's warm, busy ball,
   Whose plaintive cry is heard as she flies
   In one blue stoop from out the sties
   Into the evening's empty hall.

Oh, water-hen, beside the rushes
Hide your quaint, unfading blushes,
Still your quick tail, and lie as dead,
Till the distance folds over his ominous tread.

The rabbit presses back her ears,
Turns back her liquid, anguished eyes
And crouches low: then with wild spring
Spurts from the terror of *his* oncoming
To be choked back, the wire ring
Her frantic effort throttling:
   Piteous brown ball of quivering fears!

Ah soon in his large, hard hands she dies,
And swings all loose to the swing of his walk.
Yet calm and kindly are his eyes
And ready to open in brown surprise
Should I not answer to his talk
Or should he my tears surmise.

I hear his hand on the latch, and rise from my chair
Watching the door open: he flashes bare
His strong teeth in a smile, and flashes his eyes
In a smile like triumph upon me; then careless-wise
He flings the rabbit soft on the table board
And comes towards me: ah, the uplifted sword
Of his hand against my bosom, and oh, the broad
Blade of his hand that raises my face to applaud
His coming: he raises up my face to him
And caresses my mouth with his fingers, which still smell grim
Of the rabbit's fur! God, I am caught in a snare!
I know not what fine wire is round my throat,
I only know I let him finger there
My pulse of life, letting him nose like a stoat
Who sniffs with joy before he drinks the blood:
And down his mouth comes to my mouth, and down
His dark bright eyes descend like a fiery hood
Upon my mind: his mouth meets mine, and a flood
Of sweet fire sweeps across me, so I drown
Within him, die, and find death good.

SNAP-DRAGON

SHE bade me follow to her garden, where
The mellow sunlight stood as in a cup
Between the old grey walls; I did not dare
To raise my face, I did not dare look up,
Lest her bright eyes like sparrows should fly in
My windows of discovery, and shrill 'Sin.'

So with a downcast mien and laughing voice
I followed, followed the swing of her white dress
That rocked in a lilt along: I watched the poise
Of her feet as they flew for a space, then paused to press
The grass deep down with the royal burden of her:
And gladly I'd offered my breast to the tread of her.

'I like to see,' she said, and she crouched her down,
She sunk into my sight like a settling bird;
And her bosom couched in the confines of her gown
Like heavy birds at rest there, softly stirred
By her measured breaths: 'I like to see,' said she,
'The snap-dragon put out his tongue at me.'

She laughed, she reached her hand out to the flower,
Closing its crimson throat. My own throat in her power
Strangled, my heart swelled up so full
As if it would burst its wine-skin in my throat,
Choke me in my own crimson. I watched her pull
The gorge of the gaping flower, till the blood did float

Over my eyes, and I was blind –
Her large brown hand stretched over
The windows of my mind;
And there in the dark I did discover
Things I was out to find:
My Grail, a brown bowl twined
With swollen veins that met in the wrist,
Under whose brown the amethyst
I longed to taste. I longed to turn
My heart's red measure in her cup,
I longed to feel my hot blood burn
With the amethyst in her cup.

Then suddenly she looked up,
And I was blind in a tawny-gold day,
Till she took her eyes away.

So she came down from above
And emptied my heart of love.
So I held my heart aloft
To the cuckoo that hung like a dove,
And she settled soft.

It seemed that I and the morning world
Were pressed cup-shape to take this reiver
Bird who was weary to have furled
Her wings in us,
As we were weary to receive her.

> *This bird, this rich,*
> *Sumptuous central grain,*
> *This mutable witch,*
> *This one refrain,*
> *This laugh in the fight,*
> *This clot of night,*
> *This field of delight.*

She spoke, and I closed my eyes
To shut hallucinations out.
I echoed with surprise
Hearing my mere lips shout
The answer they did devise.

Again I saw a brown bird hover
Over the flowers at my feet;
I felt a brown bird hover
Over my heart, and sweet
Its shadow lay on my heart.
I thought I saw on the clover
A brown bee pulling apart
The closed flesh of the clover
And burrowing in its heart.

She moved her hand, and again
I felt the brown bird cover
My heart; and then
The bird came down on my heart,
As on a nest the rover
Cuckoo comes, and shoves over
The brim each careful part
Of love, takes possession, and settles her down,
With her wings and her feathers to drown
The nest in a heat of love.

She turned her flushed face to me for the glint
Of a moment. 'See,' she laughed, 'if you also
Can make them yawn.' I put my hand to the dint
In the flower's throat, and the flower gaped wide with woe.
She watched, she went of a sudden intensely still,
She watched my hand, to see what it would fulfil.

I pressed the wretched, throttled flower between
My fingers, till its head lay back, its fangs
Poised at her. Like a weapon my hand was white and keen,
And I held the choked flower-serpent in its pangs
Of mordant anguish, till she ceased to laugh,
Until her pride's flag, smitten, cleaved down to the staff.

She hid her face, she murmured between her lips
The low word 'Don't.' I let the flower fall,
But held my hand afloat towards the slips
Of blossom she fingered, and my fingers all
Put forth to her: she did not move, nor I,
For my hand like a snake watched hers, that could not fly.

Then I laughed in the dark of my heart, I did exult
Like a sudden chuckling of music. I bade her eyes
Meet mine, I opened her helpless eyes to consult
Their fear, their shame, their joy that underlies
Defeat in such a battle. In the dark of her eyes
My heart was fierce to make her laughter rise.

Till her dark deeps shook with convulsive thrills, and the dark
Of her spirit wavered like water thrilled with light;
And my heart leaped up in longing to plunge its stark
Fervour within the pool of her twilight,
Within her spacious soul, to find delight.

And I do not care, though the large hands of revenge
Shall get my throat at last, shall get it soon,
If the joy that they are lifted to avenge
Have risen red on my night as a harvest moon,
Which even death can only put out for me;
And death, I know, is better than not-to-be.

LIGHTNING

I FELT the lurch and halt of her heart
   Next my breast, where my own heart was beating;
And I laughed to feel it plunge and bound,
And strange in my blood-swept ears was the sound
   Of the words I kept repeating,
Repeating with tightened arms, and the hot blood's blindfold
     art.

Her breath flew warm against my neck,
   Warm as a flame in the close night air;
And the sense of her clinging flesh was sweet
Where her arms and my neck's blood-surge could meet.
   Holding her thus, did I care
That the black night hid her from me, blotted out every speck?

I leaned me forward to find her lips,
   And claim her utterly in a kiss,
When the lightning flew across her face,
And I saw her for the flaring space
   Of a second, afraid of the clips
Of my arms, inert with dread, wilted in fear of my kiss.

A moment, like a wavering spark,
　　Her face lay there before my breast,
Pale love lost in a snow of fear,
And guarded by a glittering tear,
　　And lips apart with dumb cries;
A moment, and she was taken again in the merciful dark.

I heard the thunder, and felt the rain,
　　And my arms fell loose, and I was dumb.
Almost I hated her, she was so good,
Hated myself, and the place, and my blood,
　　Which burned with rage, as I bade her come
Home, away home, ere the lightning floated forth again.

BALLAD OF ANOTHER OPHELIA

O H the green glimmer of apples in the orchard,
Lamps in a wash of rain!
Oh the wet walk of my brown hen through the stackyard,
Oh tears on the window pane!

Nothing now will ripen the bright green apples,
Full of disappointment and of rain,
Brackish they will taste, of tears, when the yellow dapples
Of autumn tell the withered tale again.

All round the yard it is cluck, my brown hen,
Cluck, and the rain-wet wings,
Cluck, my marigold bird, and again
Cluck for your yellow darlings.

For the grey rat found the gold thirteen
Huddled away in the dark:
Flutter for a moment, oh the beast is quick and keen,
Extinct one yellow-fluffy spark.

Once I had a lover bright like running water,
Once his face was laughing like the sky;
Open like the sky looking down in all its laughter
On the buttercups, and the buttercups was I.

What, then, is there hidden in the skirts of all the blossom?
What is peeping from your wings, oh mother hen?
'Tis the sun who asks the question, in a lovely haste for
     wisdom;
What a lovely haste for wisdom is in men!

Yea, but it is cruel when undressed is all the blossom,
And her shift is lying white upon the floor,
That a grey one, like a shadow, like a rat, a thief, a rainstorm,
Creeps upon her then and gathers in his store.

Oh the grey garner that is full of half-grown apples,
Oh the golden sparkles laid extinct!
And oh, behind the cloud-sheaves, like yellow autumn dapples,
Did you see the wicked sun that winked!

A COLLIER'S WIFE

SOMEBODY'S knocking at the door
    Mother, come down and see,
– I's think it's nobbut a beggar,
    Say, I'm busy.

It's not a beggar, mother, – hark
    How hard he knocks . . .
– Eh, tha'rt a mard-'arsed kid,
    'E'll gi'e thee socks!

Shout an' ax what 'e wants,
    I canna come down.
– 'E says 'Is it Arthur Holliday's?'
    Say 'Yes,' tha clown.

'E says, 'Tell your mother as 'er mester's
    Got hurt i' th' pit.'
What — oh my sirs, 'e never says that,
    That's niver it.

Come out o' the way an' let me see,
    Eh, there's no peace!
An' stop thy scraightin', childt,
    Do shut thy face.

'Your mester's 'ad an accident,
    An' they're ta'ein 'im i' th' ambulance
To Nottingham,' — Eh dear o' me
    If 'e's not a man for mischance!

Wheers he hurt this time, lad?
    — I dunna know,
They on'y towd me it wor bad —
    It would be so!

Eh, what a man! — an' that cobbly road,
    They'll jolt him a'most to death,
I'm sure he's in for some trouble
    Nigh every time he takes breath.

Out o' my way, childt — dear o' me, wheer
    Have I put his clean stockings and shirt;
Goodness knows if they'll be able
    To take off his pit dirt.

An' what a moan he'll make — there niver
    Was such a man for a fuss
If anything ailed him — at any rate
    I shan't have him to nuss.

I do hope it's not very bad!
    Eh, what a shame it seems
As some should ha'e hardly a smite o' trouble
    An' others has reams.

It's a shame as 'e should be knocked about
    Like this, I'm sure it is!
He's had twenty accidents, if he's had one;
    Owt bad, an' it's his.

There's one thing, we'll have peace for a bit,
    Thank Heaven for a peaceful house;
An' there's compensation, sin' it's accident,
    An' club money – I nedn't grouse.

An' a fork an' a spoon he'll want, an' what else;
    I s'll never catch that train –
What a traipse it is if a man gets hurt –
    I s'd think he'll get right again.

VIOLETS

SISTER, tha knows while we was on the planks
    Aside o' th' grave, while th' coffin wor lyin' yet
On th' yaller clay, an' th' white flowers top of it
    Tryin' to keep off 'n him a bit o' th' wet,

An' parson makin' haste, an' a' the black
    Huddlin' close together a cause o' th' rain,
Did t' 'appen ter notice a bit of a lass away back
    By a head-stun, sobbin' an' sobbin' again?

    – How should I be looking' round
      An' me standin' on the plank
    Beside the open ground,
      Where our Ted 'ud soon be sank?

Yi, an' 'im that young,
   Snapped sudden out of all
His wickedness, among
   Pals worse n'r ony name as you could call.

Let be that; there's some o' th' bad as we
   Like better nor all your good, an' 'e was one.
— An' cos I liked him best, yi, bett'r nor thee,
   I canna bide to think where he is gone.

Ah know tha liked 'im bett'r nor me. But let
   Me tell thee about this lass. When you had gone
Ah stopped behind on t' pad i' th' drippin wet
   An' watched what 'er 'ad on.

Tha should ha' seed 'er slive up when we'd gone,
   Tha should ha' seed her kneel an' look in
At th' sloppy wet grave — an' 'er little neck shone
   That white, an' 'er shook that much, I'd like to begin

Scraightin' mysen as well. 'Er undid 'er black
   Jacket at th' bosom, an' took from out of it
Over a double 'andful of violets, all in a pack
   Ravelled blue and white — warm, for a bit

O' th' smell come waftin' to me. 'Er put 'er face
   Right intil 'em and scraighted out again,
Then after a bit 'er dropped 'em down that place,
   An' I come away, because o' the teemin' rain.

WEDDING MORN

THE morning breaks like a pomegranate
   In a shining crack of red,
Ah, when to-morrow the dawn comes late
   Whitening across the bed,

It will find me watching at the marriage gate
  And waiting while light is shed
On him who is sleeping satiate,
  With a sunk, abandoned head.

And when the dawn comes creeping in,
  Cautiously I shall raise
Myself to watch the morning win
  My first of days,
As it shows him sleeping a sleep he got
  Of me, as under my gaze,
He grows distinct, and I see his hot
  Face freed of the wavering blaze.

Then I shall know which image of God
  My man is made toward,
And I shall know my bitter rod
  Or my rich reward.
And I shall know the stamp and worth
  Of the coin I've accepted as mine,
Shall see an image of heaven or of earth
  On his minted metal shine.

Yea and I long to see him sleep
  In my power utterly,
I long to know what I have to keep,
  I long to see
My love, that spinning coin, laid still
  And plain at the side of me,
For me to count — for I know he will
  Greatly enrichen me.

And then he will be mine, he will lie'
  In my power utterly,
Opening his value plain to my eye
  He will sleep of me.

He will lie negligent, resign
  His all to me, and I
Shall watch the dawn light up for me
  This sleeping wealth of mine.

And I shall watch the wan light shine
  On his sleep that is filled of me,
On his brow where the wisps of fond hair twine
  So truthfully,
On his lips where the light breaths come and go
  Naïve and winsomely,
On his limbs that I shall weep to know
  Lie under my mastery.

DREAMS OLD AND NASCENT

Old

I HAVE opened the window to warm my hands on the sill
Where the sunlight soaks in the stone: the afternoon
Is full of dreams, my love, the boys are all still
In a wistful dream of Lorna Doone.

The clink of the shunting engines is sharp and fine,
Like savage music striking far off, and there
On the great, uplifted blue palace, lights stir and shine
Where the glass is domed in the blue, soft air.

There lies the world, my darling, full of wonder and
      wistfulness and strange
Recognitions and greetings of half-acquaint things, as I greet
      the cloud
Of blue palace aloft there, among misty indefinite dreams that
      range
At the back of my life's horizon, where the dreamings of past
      lives crowd.

Over the nearness of Norwood Hill, through the mellow veil
Of the afternoon glows to me the old romance of David and
    Dora,
With the old, sweet, soothing tears, and laughter that shakes
    the sail
Of the ship of the soul over seas where dreamed dreams lure
    the unoceaned explorer.

All the bygone, hushèd years
Streaming back where the mist distils
Into forgetfulness: soft-sailing waters where fears
No longer shake, where the silk sail fills
With an unfelt breeze that ebbs over the seas, where the storm
Of living has passed, on and on
Through the coloured iridescence that swims in the warm
Wake of the tumult now spent and gone,
Drifts my boat, wistfully lapsing after
The mists of vanishing tears and the echo of laughter.

Nascent

My world is a painted fresco, where coloured shapes
Of old, ineffectual lives linger blurred and warm;
And endless tapestry the past has woven drapes
The halls of my life, compelling my soul to conform.

The surface of dreams is broken,
The picture of the past is shaken and scattered.
Fluent, active figures of men pass along the railway, and I am
    woken
From the dreams that the distance flattered.

Along the railway, active figures of men.
They have a secret that stirs in their limbs as they move
Out of the distance, nearer, commanding my dreamy world.

Here in the subtle, rounded flesh
Beats the active ecstasy.
In the sudden lifting my eyes, it is clearer,
The fascination of the quick, restless Creator moving through
    the mesh
Of men, vibrating in ecstasy through the rounded flesh.

Oh my boys, bending over your books,
In you is trembling and fusing
The creation of a new-patterned dream, dream of a generation:
And I watch to see the Creator, the power that patterns the
    dream.

The old dreams are beautiful, beloved, soft-toned, and sure,
But the dream-stuff is molten and moving mysteriously,
Alluring my eyes; for I, am I not also dream-stuff,
Am I not quickening, diffusing myself in the pattern, shaping
    and shapen?

Here in my class is the answer for the great yearning:
Eyes where I can watch the swim of old dreams reflected on
    the molten metal of dreams,
Watch the stir which is rhythmic and moves them all as a
    heart-beat moves the blood,
Here in the swelling flesh the great activity working,
Visible there in the change of eyes and the mobile features.

Oh the great mystery and fascination of the unseen Shaper,
The power of the melting, fusing Force – heat, light, all in one,
Everything great and mysterious in one, swelling and shaping
    the dream in the flesh,
As it swells and shapes a bud into blossom.

Oh the terrible ecstasy of the consciousness that I am life!
Oh the miracle of the whole, the widespread, labouring
    concentration
Swelling mankind like one bud to bring forth the fruit of a
    dream,

Oh the terror of lifting the innermost I out of the sweep of the
      impulse of life,
And watching the great Thing labouring through the whole
      round flesh of the world;
And striving to catch a glimpse of the shape of the coming
      dream,
As it quickens within the labouring, white-hot metal,
Catch the scent and the colour of the coming dream,
Then to fall back exhausted into the unconscious, molten life!

THE BEST OF SCHOOL

THE blinds are drawn because of the sun,
And the boys and the room in a colourless gloom
Of under-water float: bright ripples run
Across the walls as the blinds are blown
To let the sunlight in; and I,
As I sit on the beach of the class alone,
Watch the boys in their summer blouses,
As they write, their round heads busily bowed:
And one after another rouses
And lifts his face and looks at me,
And my eyes meet his very quietly,
Then he turns again to his work, with glee.

With glee he turns, with a little glad
Ecstasy of work he turns from me,
An ecstasy surely sweet to be had.

And very sweet while the sunlight waves
In the fresh of the morning, it is to be
A teacher of these young boys, my slaves
Only as swallows are slaves to the eaves
They build upon, as mice are slaves
To the man who threshes and sows the sheaves.

Oh, sweet it is
To feel the lads' looks light on me,
Then back in a swift, bright flutter to work,
As birds who are stealing turn and flee.

Touch after touch I feel on me
As their eyes glance at me for the grain
Of rigour they taste delightedly.

And all the class,
As tendrils reached out yearningly
Slowly rotate till they touch the tree
That they cleave unto, that they leap along
Up to their lives – so they to me.

So do they cleave and cling to me,
So I lead them up, so do they twine
Me up, caress and clothe with free
Fine foliage of lives this life of mine;
The lowest stem of this life of mine,
The old hard stem of my life
That bears aloft towards rarer skies
My top of life, that buds on high
Amid the high wind's enterprise.

They all do clothe my ungrowing life
With a rich, a thrilled young clasp of life;
A clutch of attachment, like parenthood,
Mounts up to my heart, and I find it good.

And I lift my head upon the troubled tangled world, and
    though the pain
Of living my life were doubled, I still have this to comfort and
    sustain,

I have such swarming sense of lives at the base of me, such
    sense of lives
Clustering upon me, reaching up, as each after the other strives
To follow my life aloft to the fine wild air of life and the storm
    of thought,
And though I scarcely see the boys, or know that they are
    there, distraught
As I am with living my life in earnestness, still progressively
    and alone,
Though they cling, forgotten the most part, not companions,
    scarcely known
To me – yet still because of the sense of their closeness clinging
    densely to me,
And slowly fingering up my stem and following all tinily
The way that I have gone and now am leading, they are dear to
    me.

They keep me assured, and when my soul feels lonely,
All mistrustful of thrusting its shoots where only
I alone am living, then it keeps
Me comforted to feel the warmth that creeps
Up dimly from their striving; it heartens my strife:
And when my heart is chill with loneliness,
Then comforts it the creeping tenderness
Of all the strays of life that climb my life.

AFTERNOON IN SCHOOL

The Last Lesson

WHEN will the bell ring, and end this weariness?
How long have they tugged the leash, and strained apart
My pack of unruly hounds: I cannot start
Them again on a quarry of knowledge they hate to hunt,
I can haul them and urge them no more.

45

No more can I endure to bear the brunt
Of the books that lie out on the desks: a full three score
Of several insults of blotted pages and scrawl
Of slovenly work that they have offered me.
I am sick, and tired more than any thrall
Upon the woodstacks working weariedly.

         And shall I take
The last dear fuel and heap it on my soul
Till I rouse my will like a fire to consume
Their dross of indifference, and burn the scroll
Of their insults in punishment? — I will not!
I will not waste myself to embers for them,
Not all for them shall the fires of my life be hot,
For myself a heap of ashes of weariness, till sleep
Shall have raked the embers clear: I will keep
Some of my strength for myself, for if I should sell
It all for them, I should hate them —
     — I will sit and wait for the bell.

A BABY RUNNING BAREFOOT

WHEN the bare feet of the baby beat across the grass
The little white feet nod like white flowers in the wind,
They poise and run like ripples lapping across the water;
And the sight of their white play among the grass
Is like a little robin's song, winsome,
Or as two white butterflies settle in the cup of one flower
For a moment, then away with a flutter of wings.

I long for the baby to wander hither to me
Like a wind-shadow wandering over the water,
So that she can stand on my knee
With her little bare feet in my hands,
Cool like syringa buds,
Firm and silken like pink young peony flowers.

COROT

THE trees rise tall and taller, lifted
On a subtle rush of cool grey flame
That issuing out of the dawn has sifted
    The spirit from each leaf's frame.

For the trailing, leisurely rapture of life
Drifts dimly forward, easily hidden
By bright leaves uttered aloud, and strife
    Of shapes in the grey mist chidden.

The grey, phosphorescent, pellucid advance
Of the luminous purpose of God shines out
Where the lofty trees athwart stream chance
    To shake flakes of its shadow about.

The subtle, steady rush of the whole
Grey foam-mist of advancing God,
As He silently sweeps to His somewhere, his goal,
    Is heard in the grass of the sod.

Is heard in the windless whisper of leaves
In the silent labours of men in the field,
In the downward dropping of flimsy sheaves
    Of cloud the rain skies yield.

In the tapping haste of a fallen leaf,
In the flapping of red-roof smoke, and the small
Foot-stepping tap of men beneath
    These trees so huge and tall.

For what can all sharp-rimmed substance but catch
In a backward ripple, God's purpose, reveal
For a moment His mighty direction, snatch
    A spark beneath His wheel.

Since God sweeps onward dim and vast,
Creating the channelled vein of Man
And Leaf for His passage, His shadow is cast
    On all for us to scan.

Ah listen, for Silence is not lonely:
Imitate the magnificent trees
That speak no word of their rapture, but only
    Breathe largely the luminous breeze.

END OF ANOTHER HOME-HOLIDAY

I

WHEN shall I see the half moon sink again
Behind the black sycamore at the end of the garden?
When will the scent of the dim, white phlox
Creep up the wall to me, and in at my open window?

Why is it, the long slow stroke of the midnight bell,
    (Will it never finish the twelve?)
Falls again and again on my heart with a heavy reproach?

The moon-mist is over the village, out of the mist speaks the
        bell,
And all the little roofs of the village bow low, pitiful,
        beseeching, resigned:
    Oh, little home, what is it I have not done well?

Ah home, suddenly I love you,
As I hear the sharp clean trot of a pony down the road,
Succeeding sharp little sounds dropping into the silence,
Clear upon the long-drawn hoarseness of a train across the
        valley.

The light has gone out from under my mother's door.
 That she should love me so,
 She, so lonely, greying now,
 And I leaving her,
 Bent on my pursuits!

Love is the great Asker,
The sun and the rain do not ask the secret
Of the time when the grain struggles down in the dark.
The moon walks her lonely way without anguish,
Because no loved one grieves over her departure.

2

Forever, ever by my shoulder pitiful Love will linger,
Crouching as little houses crouch under the mist when I turn.
Forever, out of the mist the church lifts up her reproachful
 finger,
Pointing my eyes in wretched defiance where love hides her
 face to mourn.

 Oh but the rain creeps down to wet the grain
 That struggles alone in the dark,
 And asking nothing, cheerfully steals back again!
 The moon sets forth o' nights
 To walk the lonely, dusky heights
 Serenely, with steps unswerving;
 Pursued by no sigh of bereavement,
 No tears of love unnerving
 Her constant tread:
 While ever at my side,
 Frail and sad, with grey bowed head,
 The beggar-woman, the yearning-eyed
 Inexorable love goes lagging.

The wild young heifer, glancing distraught,
With a strange new knocking of life at her side
 Runs seeking a loneliness.

The little grain draws down the earth to hide.
Nay, even the slumberous egg, as it labours under the shell,
  Patiently to divide, and self-divide,
Asks to be hidden, and wishes nothing to tell.

But when I draw the scanty cloak of silence over my eyes,
Piteous Love comes peering under the hood.
Touches the clasp with trembling fingers, and tries
To put her ear to the painful sob of my blood,
While her tears soak through to my breast,
        Where they burn and cauterise.

3

The moon lies back and reddens.
In the valley, a corncrake calls
        Monotonously,
With a piteous, unalterable plaint, that deadens
        My confident activity:
With a hoarse, insistent request that falls
        Unweariedly, unweariedly,
        Asking something more of me,
            Yet more of me!

THE BRIDE

MY love looks like a girl to-night,
  But she is old.
The plaits that lie along her pillow
  Are not gold,

But threaded with filigree silver,
  And uncanny cold.

She looks like a young maiden, since her brow
  Is smooth and fair,
Her cheeks are very smooth, her eyes are closed.
  She sleeps a rare
Still winsome sleep, so still, and so composed.

Nay, but she sleeps like a bride, and dreams her dreams
  Of perfect things.
She lies at last, the darling, in the shape of her dream,
  And her dead mouth sings
By its shape, like the thrushes in clear evenings.

SORROW

WHY does the thin grey strand
Floating up from the forgotten
Cigarette between my fingers,
Why does it trouble me?

Ah, you will understand;
When I carried my mother downstairs,
A few times only, at the beginning
Of her soft-foot malady,

I should find, for a reprimand
To my gaiety, a few long grey hairs
On the breast of my coat; and one by one
I watched them float up the dark chimney.

PIANO

SOFTLY, in the dusk, a woman is singing to me;
Taking me back down the vista of years, till I see
A child sitting under the piano, in the boom of the tingling
    strings
And pressing the small, poised feet of a mother who smiles as
    she sings.

In spite of myself, the insidious mastery of song
Betrays me back, till the heart of me weeps to belong
To the old Sunday evenings at home, with winter outside
And hymns in the cosy parlour, the tinkling piano our guide.

So now it is vain for the singer to burst into clamour
With the great black piano appassionato. The glamour
Of childish days is upon me, my manhood is cast
Down in the flood of remembrance, I weep like a child for the
     past.

UNDER THE OAK

You, if you were sensible,
When I tell you the stars flash signals, each one dreadful,
You would not turn and answer me
'The night is wonderful.'

Even you, if you knew
How this darkness soaks me through and through, and infuses
Unholy fear in my vapour, you would pause to distinguish
What hurts, from what amuses.

For I tell you
Beneath this powerful tree, my whole soul's fluid
Oozes away from me as a sacrifice steam
At the knife of a Druid.

Again I tell you, I bleed, I am bound with withies,
My life runs out.
I tell you my blood runs out on the floor of this oak,
Gout upon gout.

Above me springs the blood-born mistletoe
In the shady smoke.
But who are you, twittering to and fro
Beneath the oak?

What thing better are you, what worse?
What have you to do with the mysteries
Of this ancient place, of my ancient curse?
What place have you in my histories?

PARLIAMENT HILL IN THE EVENING

THE houses fade in a melt of mist
    Blotching the thick, soiled air
With reddish places that still resist
    The Night's slow care.

The hopeless, wintry twilight fades,
    The city corrodes out of sight
As the body corrodes when death invades
    That citadel of delight.

Now verdigris smoulderings softly spread
    Through the shroud of the town, as slow
Night-lights hither and thither shed
    Their ghastly glow.

THE NORTH COUNTRY

IN another country, black poplars shake themselves over a
        pond,
And rooks and the rising smoke-waves scatter and wheel from
        the works beyond;
The air is dark with north and with sulphur, the grass is a
        darker green,
And people darkly invested with purple move palpable
        through the scene.

Soundlessly down across the counties, out of the resonant
      gloom
That wraps the north in stupor and purple travels the deep,
      slow boom
Of the man-life north-imprisoned, shut in the hum of the
      purpled steel
As it spins to sleep on its motion, drugged dense in the sleep of
      the wheel.

Out of the sleep, from the gloom of motion, soundlessly,
      somnambule
Moans and booms the soul of a people imprisoned, asleep in
      the rule
Of the strong machine that runs mesmeric, booming the spell
      of its word
Upon them and moving them helpless, mechanic, their will to
      its will deferred.

Yet all the while comes the droning inaudible, out of the violet
      air,
The moaning of sleep-bound beings in travail that toil and are
      will-less there
In the spell-bound north, convulsive now with a dream near
      morning, strong
With violent achings heaving to burst the sleep that is now not
      long.

BLUE

THE earth again like a ship steams out of the dark sea over
The edge of the blue, and the sun stands up to see us glide
Slowly into another day; slowly the rover
Vessel of darkness takes the rising tide.

I, on the deck, am startled by this dawn confronting
Me who am issued amazed from the darkness, stripped
And quailing here in the sunshine, betrayed from haunting
The soundless night whereon our days are shipped.

Feeling myself undawning, the day's light playing upon me,
I who am substance of shadow, I all compact
Of the stuff of the night, finding myself all wrongly
Among the crowds of things in the sunshine jostled and racked.

I with the night on my lips, I sigh with the silence of death;
And what do I care though the very stones should cry me
    unreal, though the clouds
Shine in conceit of substance upon me, who am less than the
    rain.
Do I not know the darkness within them? What are they but
    shrouds?

The clouds go down the sky with a wealthy ease
Casting a shadow of scorn upon me for my share in death; but I
Hold my own in the midst of them, darkling, defy
The whole of the day to extinguish the shadow I lift on the
    breeze.

Yea, though the very clouds have vantage over me,
Enjoying their glancing flight, though love is dead,
I still am not homeless here, I've a tent by day
Of darkness where she sleeps on her perfect bed.

And I know the Host, the minute sparkling of darkness
Which vibrates untouched and perfect through the grandeur of
    night,
But which, when dawn crows challenge, assaulting the vivid
    motes
Of living darkness, bursts fretfully, and is bright:

      Runs like a fretted arc-lamp into light,
      Stirred by conflict to shining, which else
      Were dark and whole with the night.

Runs to a fret of speed like a racing wheel,
Which else were aslumber along with the whole
Of the dark, swinging rhythmic instead of a-reel.

Is chafed to anger, bursts into rage like thunder;
Which else were a silent grasp that held the heavens
Arrested, beating thick with wonder.

Leaps like a fountain of blue sparks leaping
In a jet from out of obscurity,
Which erst was darkness sleeping.

Runs into streams of bright blue drops,
Water and stones and stars, and myriads
Of twin-blue eyes, and crops

Of floury grain, and all the hosts of day,
All lovely hosts of ripples caused by fretting
The Darkness into play.

THE MYSTIC BLUE

OUT of the darkness, fretted sometimes in its sleeping,
Jets of sparks in fountains of blue come leaping
To sight, revealing a secret, numberless secrets keeping.

Sometimes the darkness trapped within a wheel
Runs into speed like a dream, the blue of the steel
Showing the rocking darkness now a-reel.

And out of the invisible, streams of bright blue drops
Rain from the showery heavens, and bright blue crops
Surge from the under-dark to their ladder-tops.

And all the manifold blue and joyous eyes,
The rainbow arching over in the skies,
New sparks of wonder opening in surprise

All these pure things come foam and spray of the sea
Of Darkness abundant, which shaken mysteriously,
Breaks into dazzle of living, as dolphins leap from the sea
Of midnight and shake it to fire, till the flame of the shadow
    we see.

1912—18

from *'Look! We Have Come Through!'*

BEI HENNEF

THE little river twittering in the twilight,
The wan, wandering look of the pale sky,
   This is almost bliss.

And everything shut up and gone to sleep,
All the troubles and anxieties and pain
   Gone under the twilight.

Only the twilight now, and the soft 'Sh!' of the river
   That will last for ever.

And at last I know my love for you is here;
I can see it all, it is whole like the twilight,
It is large, so large, I could not see it before,
Because of the little lights and flickers and interruptions,
   Troubles, anxieties and pains.

You are the call and I am the answer,
You are the wish, and I the fulfilment,
You are the night, and I the day.
   What else? it is perfect enough.
   It is perfectly complete,
   You and I,
   What more — ?

Strange, how we suffer in spite of this!

HENNEF AM RHEIN

FIRST MORNING

THE night was a failure
   but why not —?

In the darkness
   with the pale dawn seething at the window
   through the black frame
   I could not be free,
   not free myself from the past, those others —
   and our love was a confusion,
   there was a horror,
   you recoiled away from me.

Now, in the morning
As we sit in the sunshine on the seat by the little shrine,
And look at the mountain-walls,
Walls of blue shadow,
And see so near at our feet in the meadow
Myriads of dandelion pappus
Bubbles ravelled in the dark green grass
Held still beneath the sunshine —
It is enough, you are near —
The mountains are balanced,
The dandelion seeds stay half-submerged in the grass;
You and I together
We hold them proud and blithe
On our love.
They stand upright on our love,
Everything starts from us,
We are the source.

BEUERBERG

MUTILATION

A THICK mist-sheet lies over the broken wheat.
I walk up to my neck in mist, holding my mouth up.
Across there, a discoloured moon burns itself out.

I hold the night in horror;
I dare not turn round.

To-night I have left her alone.
They would have it I have left her for ever.

Oh my God, how it aches
Where she is cut off from me!

Perhaps she will go back to England.
Perhaps she will go back.
Perhaps we are parted for ever.

If I go on walking through the whole breadth of Germany
I come to the North Sea, or the Baltic.

Over there is Russia – Austria, Switzerland, France, in a circle!
I here in the undermist on the Bavarian road.

It aches in me.
What is England or France, far off,
But a name she might take?
I don't mind this continent stretching, the sea far away;
It aches in me for her
Like the agony of limbs cut off and aching;
Not even longing,
It is only agony.

A cripple!
Oh God, to be mutilated!
To be a cripple!

And if I never see her again?

I think, if they told me so
I could convulse the heavens with my horror.
I think I could alter the frame of things in my agony.
I think I could break the System with my heart.
I think, in my convulsion, the skies would break.

She too suffers.
But who could compel her, if she chose me against them all?
She has not chosen me finally, she suspends her choice.
Night folk, Tuatha De Danaan, dark Gods, govern her sleep,
Magnificent ghosts of the darkness, carry off her decision in
    sleep,
Leave her no choice, make her lapse me-ward, make her,
Oh Gods of the living Darkness, powers of Night.

WOLFRATSHAUSEN

A YOUNG WIFE

THE pain of loving you
Is almost more than I can bear.

I walk in fear of you.
The darkness starts up where
You stand, and the night comes through
Your eyes when you look at me.

Ah never before did I see
The shadows that live in the sun!

Now every tall glad tree
Turns round its back to the sun
And looks down on the ground, to see
The shadow it used to shun.

At the foot of each glowing thing
A night lies looking up.

Oh, and I want to sing
And dance, but I can't lift up
My eyes from the shadows: dark
They lie spilt round the cup.

What is it? – Hark
The faint fine seethe in the air!

Like the seething sound in a shell!
It is death still seething where
The wild-flower shakes its bell
And the skylark twinkles blue –

The pain of loving you
Is almost more than I can bear.

GREEN

THE dawn was apple-green,
   The sky was green wine held up in the sun,
The moon was a golden petal between.

She opened her eyes, and green
   They shone, clear like flowers undone
For the first time, now for the first time seen.

ICKING

RIVER ROSES

BY the Isar, in the twilight
We were wandering and singing,
By the Isar, in the evening
We climbed the huntsman's ladder and sat swinging
In the fir-tree overlooking the marshes,

While river met with river, and the ringing
Of their pale-green glacier-water filled the evening.

By the Isar, in the twilight
We found the dark wild roses
Hanging red at the river; and simmering
Frogs were singing, and over the river closes
Was savour of ice and roses; and glimmering
Fear was abroad. We whispered: 'No one knows us.
Let it be as the snake disposes
Here in this simmering marsh.'

KLOSTER SCHAEFTLARN

GLOIRE DE DIJON

WHEN she rises in the morning
I linger to watch her;
She spreads the bath-cloth underneath the window
And the sunbeams catch her
Glistening white on the shoulders,
While down her sides the mellow
Golden shadow glows as
She stoops to the sponge, and her swung breasts
Sway like full-blown yellow
Gloire de Dijon roses.

She drips herself with water, and her shoulders
Glisten as silver, they crumple up
Like wet and falling roses, and I listen
For the sluicing of their rain-dishevelled petals.
In the window full of sunlight
Concentrates her golden shadow
Fold on fold, until it glows as
Mellow as the glory roses.

ICKING

A DOE AT EVENING

As I went through the marshes
a doe sprang out of the corn
and flashed up the hill-side
leaving her fawn.

On the sky-line
she moved round to watch,
she pricked a fine black blotch
on the sky.

I looked at her
and felt her watching;
I became a strange being.
Still, I had my right to be there with her.

Her nimble shadow trotting
along the sky-line, she
put back her fine, level-balanced head.
And I knew her.

Ah yes, being male, is not my head hard-balanced, antlered?
Are not my haunches light?
Has she not fled on the same wind with me?
Does not my fear cover her fear?

IRSCHENHAUSEN

MISERY

Out of this oubliette between the mountains
five valleys go, five passes like gates;
three of them black in shadow, two of them bright
with distant sunshine;
and sunshine fills one high valley bed,
green grass shining, and little white houses
like quartz crystals,
little, but distinct a way off.

Why don't I go?
Why do I crawl about this pot, this oubliette, stupidly?
Why don't I go?

But where?
If I come to a pine-wood, I can't say
Now I am arrived!
What are so many straight trees to me!

STERZING

BOTH SIDES OF THE MEDAL

AND because you love me
think you you do not hate me?
Ha, since you love me
to ecstasy
it follows you hate me to ecstasy.

Because when you hear me
go down the road outside the house
you must come to the window to watch me go,
do you think it is pure worship?

Because, when I sit in the room,
here, in my own house,
and you want to enlarge yourself with this friend of mine,
such a friend as he is,
yet you cannot get beyond your awareness of me
you are held back by my being in the same world with you,
do you think it is bliss alone?
sheer harmony?

No doubt if I were dead, you must
reach into death after me,
but would not your hate reach even more madly than your
        love?
your impassioned, unfinished hate?

Since you have a passion for me,
as I for you,
does not that passion stand in your way like a Balaam's ass?
and am I not Balaam's ass
golden-mouthed occasionally?
But mostly, do you not detest my bray?

Since you are confined in the orbit of me
do you not loathe the confinement?
Is not even the beauty and peace of an orbit
an intolerable prison to you,
as it is to everybody?

But we will learn to submit
each of us to the balanced, eternal orbit
wherein we circle on our fate
in strange conjunction.

What is chaos, my love?
It is not freedom.
A disarray of falling stars coming to nought.

SONG OF A MAN WHO IS NOT LOVED

THE space of the world is immense, before me and around me;
If I turn quickly, I am terrified, feeling space surround me;
Like a man in a boat on very clear, deep water, space frightens
        and confounds me.

I see myself isolated in the universe, and wonder
What effect I can have. My hands wave under
The heavens like specks of dust that are floating asunder.

I hold myself up, and feel a big wind blowing
Me like a gadfly into the dusk, without my knowing
Whither or why or even how I am going.

67

So much there is outside me, so infinitely
Small am I, what matter if minutely
I beat my way, to be lost immediately?

How shall I flatter myself that I can do
Anything in such immensity? I am too
Little to count in the wind that drifts me through.

GLASHÜTTE

RABBIT SNARED IN THE NIGHT

WHY do you spurt and sprottle
like that, bunny?
Why should I want to throttle
you, bunny?

Yes, bunch yourself between
my knees and lie still.
Lie on me with a hot, plumb, live weight,
heavy as a stone, passive,
yet hot, waiting.

What are you waiting for?
What are you waiting for?
What is the hot, plumb weight of your desire on me?
You have a hot, unthinkable desire of me, bunny.

What is that spark
glittering at me on the unutterable darkness
of your eye, bunny?
The finest splinter of a spark
that you throw off, straight on the tinder of my nerves!

It sets up a strange fire,
a soft, most unwarrantable burning
a bale-fire mounting, mounting up in me.

'Tis not of me, bunny.
It was you engendered it,
with that fine, demoniacal spark
you jetted off your eye at me.

I did not want it,
this furnace, this draught-maddened fire
which mounts up my arms
making them swell with turgid, ungovernable strength.

'Twas not *I* that wished it,
that my fingers should turn into these flames
avid and terrible
that they are at this moment.

It must have been *your* inbreathing, gaping desire
that drew this red gush in me;
I must be reciprocating *your* vacuous, hideous passion.

It must be the want in you
that has drawn this terrible draught of white fire
up my veins as up a chimney.

It must be you who desire
this intermingling of the black and monstrous fingers of
    Moloch
in the blood-jets of your throat.

Come, you shall have your desire,
since already I am implicated with you
in your strange lust.

PARADISE RE-ENTERED

THROUGH the strait gate of passion,
Between the bickering fire
Where flames of fierce love tremble
On the body of fierce desire:

To the intoxication,
The mind, fused down like a bead,
Flees in its agitation
The flames' stiff speed:

At last to calm incandescence,
Burned clean by remorseless hate,
Now, at the day's renascence
We approach the gate.

Now, from the darkened spaces
Of fear, and of frightened faces,
Death, in our awful embraces
Approached and passed by;

We near the flame-burnt porches
Where the brands of the angels, like torches
Whirl, — in these perilous marches
Pausing to sigh;

We look back on the withering roses,
The stars, in their sun-dimmed closes,
Where 'twas given us to repose us
Sure on our sanctity;

Beautiful, candid lovers,
Burnt out of our earthy covers,
We might have nestled like plovers
In the fields of eternity.

There, sure in sinless being,
All-seen, and then all-seeing,
In us life unto death agreeing,
We might have lain.

But we storm the angel-guarded
Gates of the long-discarded
Garden, which God has hoarded
Against our pain.

The Lord of Hosts, and the Devil
Are left on Eternity's level
Field, and as victors we travel
To Eden home.

Back beyond good and evil
Return we. Eve dishevel
Your hair for the bliss-drenched revel
On our primal loam.

SONG OF A MAN WHO IS LOVED

BETWEEN her breasts is my home, between her breasts.
Three sides set on me space and fear, but the fourth side rests,
Warm in a city of strength, between her breasts.

All day long I am busy and happy at my work
I need not glance over my shoulder in fear of the terrors that
    lurk
Behind. I am fortified, I am glad at my work.

I need not look after my soul; beguile my fear
With prayer, I need only come home each night to find the
    dear
Door on the latch, and shut myself in, shut out fear.

I need only come home each night and lay
My face between her breasts;
And what of good I have given the day, my peace attests.

And what I have failed in, what I have wronged
Comes up unnamed from her body and surely
Silent tongued I am ashamed.

And I hope to spend eternity
With my face down-buried between her breasts
And my still heart full of security
And my still hands full of her breasts.

SONG OF A MAN WHO HAS COME THROUGH

NOT I, not I, but the wind that blows through me!
A fine wind is blowing the new direction of Time.
If only I let it bear me, carry me, if only it carry me!
If only I am sensitive, subtle, oh, delicate, a winged gift!
If only, most lovely of all, I yield myself and am borrowed
By the fine, fine wind that takes its course through the chaos of
      the world
Like a fine, an exquisite chisel, a wedge-blade inserted;
If only I am keen and hard like the sheer tip of a wedge
Driven by invisible blows,
The rock will split, we shall come at the wonder, we shall find
      the Hesperides.

Oh, for the wonder that bubbles into my soul,
I would be a good fountain, a good well-head,
Would blur no whisper, spoil no expression.

What is the knocking?
What is the knocking at the door in the night?
It is somebody wants to do us harm.

No, no, it is the three strange angels.
Admit them, admit them.

'SHE SAID AS WELL TO ME'

SHE said as well to me: 'Why are you ashamed?
That little bit of your chest that shows between
the gap of your shirt, why cover it up?
Why shouldn't your legs and your good strong thighs
be rough and hairy? – I'm glad they are like that.
You are shy, you silly, you silly shy thing.
Men are the shyest creatures, they never will come
out of their covers. Like any snake
slipping into its bed of dead leaves, you hurry into your clothes.
And I love you so! Straight and clean and all of a piece is the
        body of a man,
such an instrument, a spade, like a spear, or an oar,
such a joy to me –'
So she laid her hands and pressed them down my sides,
so that I began to wonder over myself, and what I was.

She said to me: 'What an instrument, your body!
single and perfectly distinct from everything else!
What a tool in the hands of the Lord!
Only God could have brought it to its shape.
It feels as if his handgrasp, wearing you
had polished you and hollowed you,
hollowed this groove in your sides, grasped you under the
        breasts
and brought you to the very quick of your form,
subtler than an old, soft-worn fiddle-bow.

'When I was a child, I loved my father's riding-whip
that he used so often.
I loved to handle it, it seemed like a near part of him.
So I did his pens, and the jasper seal on his desk.
Something seemed to surge through me when I touched them.

73

'So it is with you, but here
The joy I feel!
God knows what I feel, but it is joy!
Look, you are clean and fine and singled out!
I admire you so, you are beautiful: this clean sweep of your
    sides, this firmness, this hard mould!
I would die rather than have it injured with one scar.
I wish I could grip you like the fist of the Lord,
and have you —'

So she said, and I wondered,
feeling trammelled and hurt.
It did not make me free.

Now I say to her: 'No tool, no instrument, no God!
Don't touch me and appreciate me.
It is an infamy.
You would think twice before you touched a weasel on a fence
as it lifts its straight white throat.
Your hand would not be so flig and easy.
Nor the adder we saw asleep with her head on her shoulder,
curled up in the sunshine like a princess;
when she lifted her head in delicate, startled wonder
you did not stretch forward to caress her
though she looked rarely beautiful
and a miracle as she glided delicately away, with such dignity.
And the young bull in the field, with his wrinkled, sad face,
you are afraid if he rises to his feet,
though he is all wistful and pathetic, like a monolith arrested,
    static.

'Is there nothing in me to make you hesitate?
I tell you there is all these.
And why should you overlook them in me? —'

ELYSIUM

I HAVE found a place of loneliness
Lonelier than Lyonesse
Lovelier than Paradise;

Full of sweet stillness
That no noise can transgress
Never a lamp distress.

The full moon sank in state.
I saw her stand and wait
For her watchers to shut the gate.

Then I found myself in a wonderland
All of shadow and of bland
Silence hard to understand.

I waited therefore; then I knew
The presence of the flowers that grew
Noiseless, their wonder noiseless blew.

And flashing kingfishers that flew
In sightless beauty, and the few
Shadows the passing wild-beast threw.

And Eve approaching over the ground
Unheard and subtle, never a sound
To let me know that I was found.

Invisible the hands of Eve
Upon me travelling to reeve
Me from the matrix, to relieve

Me from the rest! Ah terribly
Between the body of life and me
Her hands slid in and set me free.

Ah, with a fearful, strange detection
She found the source of my subjection
To the All, and severed the connection.

Delivered helpless and amazed
From the womb of the All, I am waiting, dazed
For memory to be erased.

Then I shall know the Elysium
That lies outside the monstrous womb
Of time from out of which I come.

CRAVING FOR SPRING

I WISH it were spring in the world.

Let it be spring!
Come, bubbling, surging tide of sap!
Come, rush of creation!
Come, life! surge through this mass of mortification!
Come, sweep away these exquisite, ghastly first-flowers,
which are rather last-flowers!
Come, thaw down their cool portentousness, dissolve them;
snowdrops, straight, death-veined exhalations of white and
        purple crocuses,
flowers of the penumbra, issue of corruption, nourished in
        mortification,
jets of exquisite finality;
Come, spring, make havoc of them!

I trample on the snowdrops, it gives me pleasure to tread down
        the jonquils,
to destroy the chill Lent lilies;
for I am sick of them, their faint-bloodedness,
slow-blooded, icy-fleshed, portentous.

I want the fine, kindling wine-sap of spring,
gold, and of inconceivably fine, quintessential brightness,
rare almost as beams, yet overwhelmingly potent,
strong like the greatest force of world-balancing.

This is the same that picks up the harvest of wheat
and rocks it, tons of grain, on the ripening wind;
the same that dangles the globe-shaped pleiads of fruit
temptingly in mid-air, between a playful thumb and finger;
oh, and suddenly, from out of nowhere, whirls the
    pear-bloom,
upon us, and apple- and almond- and apricot- and
    quince-blossom,
storms and cumulus clouds of all imaginable blossom
about our bewildered faces,
though we do not worship.

I wish it were spring
cunningly blowing on the fallen sparks, odds and ends of the
    old, scattered fire,
and kindling shapely little conflagrations
curious long-legged foals, and wide-eared calves, and naked
    sparrow-bubs.

I wish that spring
would start the thundering traffic of feet
new feet on the earth, beating with impatience.

I wish it were spring, thundering
delicate, tender spring.
I wish these brittle, frost-lovely flowers of passionate,
    mysterious corruption
were not yet to come still more from the still-flickering
    discontent.

Oh, in the spring, the bluebell bows him down for very
    exuberance,
exulting with secret warm excess,
bowed down with his inner magnificence!

Oh, yes, the gush of spring is strong enough
to toss the globe of earth like a ball on a water-jet
dancing sportfully;
as you see a tiny celluloid ball tossing on a squirt of water
for men to shoot at, penny-a-time, in a booth at a fair.

The gush of spring is strong enough
to play with the globe of earth like a ball on a fountain;
At the same time it opens the tiny hands of the hazel
with such infinite patience.

The power of the rising, golden, all-creative sap could take the
    earth
and heave it off among the stars, into the invisible;
the same sets the throstle at sunset on a bough
singing against the blackbird;
comes out in the hesitating tremor of the primrose,
and betrays its candour in the round white strawberry flower,
is dignified in the foxglove, like a Red-Indian brave.

Ah come, come quickly, spring!
Come and lift us towards our culmination, we myriads;
we who have never flowered, like patient cactuses.
Come and lift us to our end, to blossom, bring us to our
    summer
we who are winter-weary in the winter of the world.
Come making the chaffinch nests hollow and cosy,
come and soften the willow buds till they are puffed and
    furred,
then blow them over with gold.
Come and cajole the gawky colt's-foot flowers.

Come quickly, and vindicate us
against too much death.
Come quickly, and stir the rotten globe of the world from
    within,
burst it with germination, with world anew.
Come now, to us, your adherents, who cannot flower from the
    ice.
All the world gleams with the lilies of Death the
    Unconquerable,
but come, give us our turn.
Enough of the virgins and lilies, of passionate, suffocating
    perfume of corruption,
no more narcissus perfume, lily harlots, the blades of sensation
piercing the flesh to blossom of death.
Have done, have done with this shuddering, delicious business
of thrilling ruin in the flesh, of pungent passion, of rare,
    death-edged ecstasy.
Give us our turn, give us a chance, let our hour strike,
O soon, soon!

Let the darkness turn violet with rich dawn.
Let the darkness be warmed, warmed through to a ruddy
    violet,
incipient purpling towards summer in the world of the heart of
    man.

Are the violets already here!
Show me! I tremble so much to hear it, that even now
on the threshold of spring, I fear I shall die.
Show me the violets that are out.

Oh, if it be true, and the living darkness of the blood of man is
    purpling with violets,
if the violets are coming out from under the rack of men,
    winter-rotten and fallen
we shall have spring.
Pray not to die on this Pisgah blossoming with violets.
Pray to live through.

If you catch a whiff of violets from the darkness of the shadow
     of man
it will be spring in the world,
it will be spring in the world of the living;
wonderment organising itself, heralding itself with the violets,
stirring of new seasons.

Ah, do not let me die on the brink of such anticipation!
Worse, let me not deceive myself.

ZENNOR

from *Bay*

AFTER THE OPERA

DOWN the stone stairs
Girls with their large eyes wide with tragedy
Lift looks of shocked and momentous emotions up at me.
And I smile.

Ladies
Stepping like birds with their bright and pointed feet
Peer anxiously forth, as if for a boat to carry them out of the
     wreckage,
And among the wreck of the theatre crowd
I stand and smile.

They take tragedy so becomingly.
Which pleases me.

But when I meet the weary eyes
The reddened aching eyes of the bar-man with thin arms,
I am glad to go back where I came from.

✿

1920—23

✿

from *Birds, Beasts and Flowers*

TROPIC

SUN, dark sun,
Sun of black void heat,
Sun of the torrid mid-day's horrific darkness:

Behold my hair twisting and going black.
Behold my eyes turn tawny yellow
Negroid;
See the milk of northern spume
Coagulating and going black in my veins
Aromatic as frankincense.

Columns dark and soft,
Sunblack men,
Soft shafts, sunbreathing mouths,
Eyes of yellow, golden sand
As frictional, as perilous, explosive as brimstone.

Rock, waves of dark heat;
Waves of dark heat, rock, sway upwards,
Waver perpendicular.

What is the horizontal rolling of water
Compared to the flood of black heat that rolls upwards past
     my eyes?

TAORMINA

PEACE

PEACE is written on the doorstep
In lava.

Peace, black peace congealed.
My heart will know no peace
Till the hill bursts.

Brilliant, intolerable lava,
Brilliant as a powerful burning-glass,
Walking like a royal snake down the mountain towards the
      sea.

Forests, cities, bridges
Gone again in the bright trail of lava.
Naxos thousands of feet below the olive-roots,
And now the olive leaves thousands of feet below the lava fire.

Peace congealed in black lava on the doorstep.
Within, white-hot lava, never at peace
Till it burst forth blinding, withering the earth;
To set again into rock,
Grey-black rock.

Call it Peace?

TAORMINA

SOUTHERN NIGHT

COME up, thou red thing.
Come up, and be called a moon.

The mosquitoes are biting to-night
Like memories.

Memories, northern memories,
Bitter-stinging white world that bore us
Subsiding into this night.

Call it moonrise
This red anathema?

Rise, thou red thing,
Unfold slowly upwards, blood-dark;
Burst the night's membrane of tranquil stars
Finally.

Maculate
The red Macula.

TAORMINA

HUMMING-BIRD

I CAN imagine, in some otherworld
Primeval-dumb, far back
In that most awful stillness, that only gasped and hummed,
Humming-birds raced down the avenues.

Before anything had a soul,
While life was a heave of Matter, half inanimate,
This little bit chipped off in brilliance
And went whizzing through the slow, vast, succulent stems.

I believe there were no flowers, then,
In the world where the humming-bird flashed ahead of
    creation.
I believe he pierced the slow vegetable veins with his long
    beak.

Probably he was big
As mosses, and little lizards, they say were once big.
Probably he was a jabbing, terrifying monster.

We look at him through the wrong end of the long telescope of
    Time,
Luckily for us.

ESPAÑOLA

THE MOSQUITO

WHEN did you start your tricks,
Monsieur?

What do you stand on such high legs for?
Why this length of shredded shank,
You exaltation?

Is it so that you shall lift your centre of gravity upwards
And weigh no more than air as you alight upon me,
Stand upon me weightless, you phantom?

I heard a woman call you the Winged Victory
In sluggish Venice.
You turn your head towards your tail, and smile.

How can you put so much devilry
Into that translucent phantom shred
Of a frail corpus?

Queer, with your thin wings and your streaming legs
How you sail like a heron, or a dull clot of air,
A nothingness.

Yet what an aura surrounds you;
Your evil little aura, prowling, and casting a numbness on my
    mind.

That is your trick, your bit of filthy magic:
Invisibility, and the anæsthetic power
To deaden my attention in your direction.

But I know your game now, streaky sorcerer.

Queer, how you stalk and prowl the air
In circles and evasions, enveloping me,
Ghoul on wings
Winged Victory.

Settle, and stand on long thin shanks
Eyeing me sideways, and cunningly conscious that I am aware,
You speck.

I hate the way you lurch off sideways into air
Having read my thoughts against you.

Come then, let us play at unawares,
And see who wins in this sly game of bluff,
Man or mosquito.

You don't know that I exist, and I don't know that you exist.
Now then!

It is your trump,
It is your hateful little trump,
You pointed fiend,
Which shakes my sudden blood to hatred of you:
It is your small, high, hateful bugle in my ear.

Why do you do it?
Surely it is bad policy.

They say you can't help it.

If that is so, then I believe a little in Providence protecting the
        innocent.
But it sounds so amazingly like a slogan,
A yell of triumph as you snatch my scalp.

Blood, red blood
Super-magical
Forbidden liquor.

I behold you stand
For a second enspasmed in oblivion,
Obscenely ecstasied
Sucking live blood,
My blood.

Such silence, such suspended transport,
Such gorging,
Such obscenity of trespass.

You stagger
As well as you may.
Only your accursed hairy frailty,
Your own imponderable weightlessness
Saves you, wafts you away on the very draught my anger
        makes in its snatching.

Away with a pæan of derision,
You winged blood-drop.

Can I not overtake you?
Are you one too many for me,
Winged Victory?
Am I not mosquito enough to out-mosquito you?

Queer, what a big stain my sucked blood makes
Beside the infinitesimal faint smear of you!
Queer, what a dim dark smudge you have disappeared into!

SIRACUSA

CYPRESSES

TUSCAN cypresses,
What is it?

Folded in like a dark thought
For which the language is lost,
Tuscan cypresses,
Is there a great secret?
Are our words no good?

The undeliverable secret,
Dead with a dead race and a dead speech, and yet
Darkly monumental in you,
Etruscan cypresses.

Ah, how I admire your fidelity,
Dark cypresses!

Is it the secret of the long-nosed Etruscans?
The long-nosed, sensitive-footed, subtly-smiling Etruscans,
Who made so little noise outside the cypress groves?

Among the sinuous, flame-tall cypresses
That swayed their length of darkness all around
Etruscan-dusky, wavering men of old Etruria:
Naked except for fanciful long shoes,
Going with insidious, half-smiling quietness
And some of Africa's imperturbable sang-froid
About a forgotten business.

What business, then?
Nay, tongues are dead, and words are hollow as hollow
        seed-pods,
Having shed their sound and finished all their echoing
Etruscan syllables,
That had the telling.

Yet more I see you darkly concentrate,
Tuscan cypresses,
On one old thought:
On one old slim imperishable thought, while you remain
Etruscan cypresses;
Dusky, slim marrow-thought of slender, flickering men of
      Etruria,
Whom Rome called vicious.

Vicious, dark cypresses:
Vicious, you supple, brooding, softly-swaying pillars of dark
      flame.
Monumental to a dead, dead race
Embalmed in you!

Were they then vicious, the slender, tender-footed,
Long-nosed men of Etruria?
Or was their way only evasive and different, dark, like
      cypress-trees in a wind?

They are dead, with all their vices,
And all that is left
Is the shadowy monomania of some cypresses
And tombs.

The smile, the subtle Etruscan smile still lurking
Within the tombs,
Etruscan cypresses.
He laughs longest who laughs last;
Nay, Leonardo only bungled the pure Etruscan smile.

What would I not give
To bring back the rare and orchid-like
Evil-yclept Etruscan?

For as to the evil
We have only Roman word for it,
Which I, being a little weary of Roman virtue,
Don't hang much weight on.

For oh, I know, in the dust where we have buried
The silenced races and all their abominations,
We have buried so much of the delicate magic of life.

There in the deeps
That churn the frankincense and ooze the myrrh,
Cypress shadowy,
Such an aroma of lost human life!

They say the fit survive,
But I invoke the spirits of the lost.
Those that have not survived, the darkly lost,
To bring their meaning back into life again,
Which they have taken away
And wrapt inviolable in soft cypress-trees,
Etruscan cypresses.

Evil, what is evil?
There is only one evil, to deny life
As Rome denied Etruria
And mechanical America Montezuma still.

FIESOLE

Fruits

POMEGRANATE

YOU tell me I am wrong.
Who are you, who is anybody to tell me I am wrong?
I am not wrong.

In Syracuse, rock left bare by the viciousness of Greek women,
No doubt you have forgotten the pomegranate-trees in flower,
Oh so red, and such a lot of them.

Whereas at Venice
Abhorrent, green, slippery city
Whose Doges were old, and had ancient eyes,
In the dense foliage of the inner garden
Pomegranates like bright green stone,
And barbed, barbed with a crown.
Oh, crown of spiked green metal
Actually growing!

Now in Tuscany,
Pomegranates to warm your hands at;
And crowns, kingly, generous, tilting crowns
Over the left eyebrow.

And, if you dare, the fissure!

Do you mean to tell me you will see no fissure?
Do you prefer to look on the plain side?

For all that, the setting suns are open.
The end cracks open with the beginning:
Rosy, tender, glittering within the fissure.

Do you mean to tell me there should be no fissure?
No glittering, compact drops of dawn?
Do you mean it is wrong, the gold-filmed skin, integument,
    shown ruptured?

For my part, I prefer my heart to be broken.
It is so lovely, dawn-kaleidoscopic within the crack.

SAN GERVASIO IN TUSCANY

PEACH

Would you like to throw a stone at me?
Here, take all that's left of my peach.

Blood-red, deep;
Heaven knows how it came to pass.
Somebody's pound of flesh rendered up.

Wrinkled with secrets
And hard with the intention to keep them.

Why, from silvery peach-bloom,
From that shallow-silvery wine-glass on a short stem
This rolling, dropping, heavy globule?

I am thinking, of course, of the peach before I ate it.

Why so velvety, why so voluptuous heavy?
Why hanging with such inordinate weight?
Why so indented?

Why the groove?
Why the lovely, bivalve roundnesses?
Why the ripple down the sphere?
Why the suggestion of incision?

Why was not my peach round and finished like a billiard ball?
It would have been if man had made it.
Though I've eaten it now.

But it wasn't round and finished like a billiard ball.
And because I say so, you would like to throw something at
    me.

Here, you can have my peach stone.

                                        SAN GERVASIO

93

MEDLARS AND SORB-APPLES

I LOVE you, rotten,
Delicious rottenness.

I love to suck you out from your skins
So brown and soft and coming suave,
So morbid, as the Italians say.

What a rare, powerful, reminiscent flavour
Comes out of your falling through the stages of decay:
Stream within stream.

Something of the same flavour as Syracusan muscat wine
Or vulgar Marsala.

Though even the word Marsala will smack of preciosity
Soon in the pussy-foot West.

What is it?
What is it, in the grape-turning-raisin,
In the medlar, in the sorb-apple,
Wineskins of brown morbidity,
Autumnal excrementa;
What is it that reminds us of white gods?

Gods nude as blanched nut-kernels,
Strangely, half sinisterly flesh-fragrant
As if with sweat,
And drenched with mystery.

Sorb-apples, medlars with dead crowns.

I say, wonderful are the hellish experiences,
Orphic, delicate
Dionysos of the Underworld.

A kiss, and a spasm of farewell, a moment's orgasm of rupture
Then along the damp road alone, till the next turning.

And there, a new partner, a new parting, a new unfusing into
    twain,
A new gasp of further isolation,
A new intoxication of loneliness, among decaying, frost-cold
    leaves.

Going down the strange lanes of hell, more and more intensely
    alone,
The fibres of the heart parting one after the other
And yet the soul continuing, naked-footed, ever more vividly
    embodied
Like a flame blown whiter and whiter
In a deeper and deeper darkness
Ever more exquisite, distilled in separation.

So, in the strange retorts of medlars and sorb-apples
The distilled essence of hell.
The exquisite odour of leave-taking.
    Jamque vale!
Orpheus, and the winding, leaf-clogged, silent lanes of hell.

Each soul departing with its own isolation,
Strangest of all strange companions,
And best.

Medlars, sorb-apples
More than sweet
Flux of autumn
Sucked out of your empty bladders
And sipped down, perhaps, with a sip of Marsala
So that the rambling, sky-dropped grape can add its music to
    yours,
Orphic farewell, and farewell, and farewell
And the *ego sum* of Dionysos
The *sono io* of perfect drunkenness
Intoxication of final loneliness.

                                        SAN GERVASIO

FIGS

THE proper way to eat a fig, in society,
Is to split it in four, holding it by the stump,
And open it, so that it is a glittering, rosy, moist, honied,
    heavy-petalled four-petalled flower.

Then you throw away the skin
Which is just like a four-sepalled calyx,
After you have taken off the blossom with your lips.

But the vulgar way
Is just to put your mouth to the crack, and take out the flesh in
    one bite.

Every fruit has its secret.

The fig is a very secretive fruit.
As you see it standing growing, you feel at once it is symbolic:
And it seems male.
But when you come to know it better, you agree with the
    Romans, it is female.

The Italians vulgarly say, it stands for the female part; the
    fig-fruit:
The fissure, the yoni,
The wonderful moist conductivity towards the centre.

Involved,
Inturned,
The flowering all inward and womb-fibrilled;
And but one orifice.

The fig, the horse-shoe, the squash-blossom.
Symbols.

There was a flower that flowered inward, womb-ward;
Now there is a fruit like a ripe womb.

It was always a secret.
That's how it should be, the female should always be secret.

There never was any standing aloft and unfolded on a bough
Like other flowers, in a revelation of petals;
Silver-pink peach, venetian green glass of medlars and
      sorb-apples,
Shallow wine-cups on short, bulging stems
Openly pledging heaven:
Here's to the thorn in flower! Here is to Utterance!
The brave, adventurous rosaceæ.

Folded upon itself, and secret unutterable,
And milky-sapped, sap that curdles milk and makes *ricotta*,
Sap that smells strange on your fingers, that even goats won't
      taste it;
Folded upon itself, enclosed like any Mohammedan woman,
Its nakedness all within-walls, its flowering forever unseen,
One small way of access only, and this close-curtained from
      the light;
Fig, fruit of the female mystery, covert and inward,
Mediterranean fruit, with your covert nakedness,
Where everything happens invisible, flowering and
      fertilisation, and fruiting
In the inwardness of your you, that eye will never see
Till it's finished, and you're over-ripe, and you burst to give up
      your ghost.

Till the drop of ripeness exudes,
And the year is over.

And then the fig has kept her secret long enough.
So it explodes, and you see through the fissure the scarlet.
And the fig is finished, the year is over.

That's how the fig dies, showing her crimson through the
      purple slit
Like a wound, the exposure of her secret, on the open day.
Like a prostitute, the bursten fig, making a show of her secret.

That's how women die too.

The year is fallen over-ripe,
The year of our women.
The year of our women is fallen over-ripe.
The secret is laid bare.
And rottenness soon sets in.
The year of our women is fallen over-ripe.

When Eve once knew *in her mind* that she was naked
She quickly sewed fig-leaves, and sewed the same for the man.
She'd been naked all her days before,
But till then, till that apple of knowledge, she hadn't had the
      fact on her mind.

She got the fact on her mind, and quickly sewed fig-leaves.
And women have been sewing ever since.
But now they stitch to adorn the bursten fig, not to cover it.
They have their nakedness more than ever on their mind,
And they won't let us forget it.

Now, the secret
Becomes an affirmation through moist, scarlet lips
That laugh at the Lord's indignation.

What then, good Lord! cry the women.
We have kept our secret long enough.
We are a ripe fig.
Let us burst into affirmation.

They forget, ripe figs won't keep.
Ripe figs won't keep.

Honey-white figs of the north, black figs with scarlet inside, of
 the south.
Ripe figs won't keep, won't keep in any clime.
What then, when women the world over have all bursten into
 affirmation?
And bursten figs won't keep?

SAN GERVASIO

GRAPES

So many fruits come from roses
From the rose of all roses
From the unfolded rose
Rose of all the world.

Admit that apples and strawberries and peaches and pears and
 blackberries
Are all Rosaceæ,
Issue of the explicit rose,
The open-countenanced, skyward-smiling rose.

What then of the vine?
Oh, what of the tendrilled vine?

Ours is the universe of the unfolded rose,
The explicit
The candid revelation.

But long ago, oh, long ago
Before the rose began to simper supreme,
Before the rose of all roses, rose of all the world, was even in
 bud,
Before the glaciers were gathered up in a bunch out of the
 unsettled seas and winds,
Or else before they had been let down again, in Noah's flood,
There was another world, a dusky, flowerless, tendrilled world
And creatures webbed and marshy,

And on the margin, men soft-footed and pristine,
Still, and sensitive, and active,
Audile, tactile sensitiveness as of a tendril which orientates and
      reaches out,
Reaching out and grasping by an instinct more delicate than
      the moon's as she feels for the tides.

Of which world, the vine was the invisible rose,
Before petals spread, before colour made its disturbance,
      before eyes saw too much.

In a green, muddy, web-foot, unutterably songless world
The vine was rose of all roses.

There were no poppies or carnations,
Hardly a greenish lily, watery faint.
Green, dim, invisible flourishing of vines
Royally gesticulate.

Look now even now, how it keeps its power of invisibility!
Look how black, how blue-black, how globed in Egyptian
      darkness
Dropping among his leaves, hangs the dark grape!
See him there, the swart, so palpably invisible:
Whom shall we ask about him?

The negro might know a little.
When the vine was rose, Gods were dark-skinned.
Bacchus is a dream's dream.
Once God was all negroid, as now he is fair.
But it's so long ago, the ancient Bushman has forgotten more
      utterly than we, who have never known.

For we are on the brink of re-remembrance.
Which, I suppose, is why America has gone dry.
Our pale day is sinking into twilight,
And if we sip the wine, we find dreams coming upon us
Out of the imminent night.

Nay, we find ourselves crossing the fern-scented frontiers
Of the world before the floods, where man was dark and
    evasive
And the tiny vine-flower rose of all roses, perfumed,
And all in naked communion communicating as now our
    clothed vision can never communicate.
Vistas, down dark avenues
As we sip the wine.

The grape is swart, the avenues dusky and tendrilled, subtly
    prehensile,
But we, as we start awake, clutch at our vistas democratic,
    boulevards, tram-cars, policemen.
Give us our own back,
Let us go to the soda-fountain, to get sober.

Soberness, sobriety.
It is like the agonised perverseness of a child heavy with sleep,
    yet fighting, fighting to keep awake;
Soberness, sobriety, with heavy eyes propped open.

Dusky are the avenues of wine,
And we must cross the frontiers, though we will not,
Of the lost, fern-scented world:
Take the fern-seed on our lips,
Close the eyes, and go
Down the tendrilled avenues of wine and the otherworld

SAN GERVASIO

● ● ●

THE REVOLUTIONARY

LOOK at them standing there in authority,
The pale-faces,
As if it could have any effect any more.

Pale-face authority,
Caryatids,
Pillars of white bronze standing rigid, lest the skies fall.

What a job they've got to keep it up.
Their poor, idealist foreheads naked capitals
To the entablature of clouded heaven.

When the skies are going to fall, fall they will
In a great chute and rush of débâcle downwards.

Oh and I wish the high and super-gothic heavens would come
      down now,
The heavens above, that we yearn to and aspire to.

I do not yearn, nor aspire, for I am a blind Samson.
And what is daylight to me that I should look skyward?
Only I grope among you, pale-faces, caryatids, as among a
      forest of pillars that hold up the dome of high ideal
      heaven.
Which is my prison,
And all these human pillars of loftiness, going stiff,
      metallic-stunned with the weight of their responsibility
I stumble against them.
Stumbling-blocks, painful ones.

To keep on holding up this ideal civilisation
Must be excruciating: unless you stiffen into metal, when it is
      easier to stand stock rigid than to move.

This is why I tug at them, individually, with my arm round
      their waist,
The human pillars.
They are not stronger than I am, blind Samson.
The house sways.

I shall be so glad when it comes down.
I am so tired of the limitations of their Infinite.
I am so sick of the pretensions of the Spirit.
I am so weary of pale-face importance.

Am I not blind, at the round-turning mill?
Then why should I fear their pale faces?
Or love the effulgence of their holy light,
The sun of their righteousness?

To me, all faces are dark,
All lips are dusky and valved.

Save your lips, O pale-faces,
Which are slips of metal,
Like slits in an automatic-machine, you columns of
    give-and-take.

To me, the earth rolls ponderously, superbly
Coming my way without forethought or afterthought.
To me, men's footfalls fall with a dull, soft rumble, ominous
    and lovely,
Coming my way.

But not your foot-falls, pale-faces,
They are a clicketing of bits of disjointed metal
Working in motion.

To me, men are palpable, invisible nearnesses in the dark
Sending out magnetic vibrations of warning, pitch-dark throbs
    of invitation.
But you, pale-faces,
You are painful, harsh-surfaced pillars that give off nothing
    except rigidity,
And I jut against you if I try to move, for you are everywhere,
    and I am blind,
Sightless among all your visuality,
You staring caryatids.

See if I don't bring you down, and all your high opinion
And all your ponderous roofed-in erection of right and wrong,
Your particular heavens,
With a smash.

See if your skies aren't falling!
And my head, at least, is thick enough to stand it, the smash.

See if I don't move under a dark and nude, vast heaven
When your world is in ruins, under your fallen skies.
Caryatids, pale-faces.
See if I am not Lord of the dark and moving hosts
Before I die.

FLORENCE

ST MATTHEW

THEY are not all beasts.
One is a man, for example, and one is a bird.

I, Matthew, am a man.

'And I, if I be lifted up, will draw all men unto me' —

That is Jesus.
But then Jesus was not quite a man.
He was the Son of Man
Filius Meus, O remorseless logic
Out of His own mouth.

I, Matthew, being a man
Cannot be lifted up, the Paraclete
To draw all men unto me,
Seeing I am on a par with all men.

I, on the other hand,
Am drawn to the Uplifted, as all men are drawn,
To the Son of Man
Filius Meus.

Wilt thou lift me up, Son of Man?
How my heart beats!
I am man.

I am man, and therefore my heart beats, and throws the dark
      blood from side to side
All the time I am lifted up.

Yes, even during my uplifting.

And if it ceased?
If it ceased, I should be no longer man
As I am, if my heart in uplifting ceased to beat, to toss the dark
      blood from side to side, causing my myriad secret
      streams.

After the cessation
I might be a soul in bliss, an angel, approximating to the
      Uplifted;
But that is another matter;
I am Matthew, the man,
And I am not that other angelic matter.

So I will be lifted up, Saviour,
But put me down again in time, Master,
Before my heart stops beating, and I become what I am not.
Put me down again on the earth, Jesus, on the brown soil
Where flowers sprout in the acrid humus, and fade into humus
      again.
Where beasts drop their unlicked young, and pasture, and
      drop their droppings among the turf.
Where the adder darts horizontal.

Down on the damp, unceasing ground, where my feet belong
And even my heart, Lord, forever, after all uplifting;
The crumbling, damp, fresh land, life horizontal and ceaseless.

Matthew I am, the man.
And I take the wings of the morning, to Thee, Crucified,
    Glorified.
But while flowers club their petals at evening
And rabbits make pills among the short grass
And long snakes quickly glide into the dark hole in the wall,
    hearing man approach,
I must be put down, Lord, in the afternoon,
And at evening I must leave off my wings of the spirit
As I leave off my braces,
And I must resume my nakedness like a fish, sinking down the
    dark reversion of night
Like a fish seeking the bottom, Jesus,
ΙΧΘΥΣ
Face downwards
Veering slowly
Down between the steep slopes of darkness, fucus-dark,
    seaweed-fringed valleys of the waters under the sea,
Over the edge of the soundless cataract
Into the fathomless, bottomless pit
Where my soul falls in the last throes of bottomless
    convulsion, and is fallen
Utterly beyond Thee, Dove of the Spirit;
Beyond everything, except itself.

Nay, Son of Man, I have been lifted up.
To Thee I rose like a rocket ending in mid-heaven.
But even Thou, Son of Man, canst not quaff out the dregs of
    terrestrial manhood!
They fall back from Thee.

They fall back, and like a dripping of quicksilver taking the
    downward track,
Break into drops, burn into drops of blood, and dropping,
    dropping take wing
Membraned, blood-veined wings.
On fans of unsuspected tissue, like bats
They thread and thrill and flicker ever downward
To the dark zenith of Thine antipodes
Jesus Uplifted.

Bat-winged heart of man,
Reversed flame
Shuddering a strange way down the bottomless pit
To the great depths of its reversèd zenith.

Afterwards, afterwards
Morning comes, and I shake the dews of night from the wings
    of my spirit
And mount like a lark, Beloved.

But remember, Saviour,
That my heart which like a lark at heaven's gate singing,
    hovers morning-bright to Thee,
Throws still the dark blood back and forth
In the avenues where the bat hangs sleeping, upside-down
And to me undeniable, Jesus.

Listen, Paraclete.
I can no more deny the bat-wings of my fathom-flickering
    spirit of darkness
Than the wings of the Morning and Thee, Thou Glorified.

I am Matthew, the Man:
It is understood.
And Thou art Jesus, Son of Man
Drawing all men unto Thee, but bound to release them when
    the hour strikes.

I have been, and I have returned.
I have mounted up on the wings of the morning, and I have
    dredged down to the zenith's reversal.
Which is my way, being man.
Gods may stay in mid-heaven, the Son of Man has climbed to
    the Whitsun zenith,
But I, Matthew, being a man
Am a traveller back and forth.
So be it.

TURKEY-COCK

You ruffled black blossom,
You glossy dark wind.

Your sort of gorgeousness,
Dark and lustrous
And skinny repulsive
And poppy-glossy,
Is the gorgeousness that evokes my most puzzled admiration.

Your aboriginality
Deep, unexplained,
Like a Red Indian darkly unfinished and aloof,
Seems like the black and glossy seeds of countless centuries.

Your wattles are the colour of steel-slag which has been
    red-hot
And is going cold,
Cooling to a powdery, pale-oxidised sky-blue.

Why do you have wattles, and a naked, wattled head?
Why do you arch your naked-set eye with a more-
    than-comprehensible arrogance?

The vulture is bald, so is the condor, obscenely,
But only you have thrown this amazing mantilla of oxidised
    sky-blue
And hot red over you.

This queer dross shawl of blue and vermilion,
Whereas the peacock has a diadem.

I wonder why.
Perhaps it is a sort of uncanny decoration, a veil of loose skin.
Perhaps it is your assertion, in all this ostentation, of raw
    contradictoriness.
Your wattles drip down like a shawl to your breast
And the point of your mantilla drops across your nose,
    unpleasantly.

Or perhaps it is something unfinished
A bit of slag still adhering, after your firing in the furnace of
    creation.

Or perhaps there is something in your wattles of a bull's
    dew-lap
Which slips down like a pendulum to balance the throbbing
    mass of a generous breast,
The over-drip of a great passion hanging in the balance.
Only yours would be a raw, unsmelted passion, that will not
    quite fuse from the dross.

You contract yourself,
You arch yourself as an archer's bow
Which quivers indrawn as you clench your spine
Until your veiled head almost touches backward
To the root-rising of your erected tail.
And one intense and backward-curving frisson
Seizes you as you clench yourself together
Like some fierce magnet bringing its poles together.

Burning, pale positive pole of your wattled head!
And from the darkness of that opposite one
The upstart of your round-barred, sun-round tail!

Whilst between the two, along the tense arch of your back
Blows the magnetic current in fierce blasts,
Ruffling black, shining feathers like lifted mail,
Shuddering storm wind, or a water rushing through.

Your brittle, super-sensual arrogance
Tosses the crape of red across your brow and down your
    breast
As you draw yourself upon yourself in insistence.

It is a declaration of such tension in will
As time has not dared to avouch, nor eternity been able to
    unbend
Do what it may.
A raw American will, that has never been tempered by life;
You brittle, will-tense bird with a foolish eye.

The peacock lifts his rods of bronze
And struts blue-brilliant out of the far East.
But watch a turkey prancing low on earth
Drumming his vaulted wings, as savages drum
Their rhythms on long-drawn, hollow, sinister drums.
The ponderous, sombre sound of the great drum of
    Huichilobos
In pyramid Mexico, during sacrifice.
Drum, and the turkey onrush,
Sudden, demonic dauntlessness, full abreast,
All the bronze gloss of all his myriad petals
Each one apart and instant.
Delicate frail crescent of the gentle outline of white
At each feather-tip
So delicate;
Yet the bronze wind-bell suddenly clashing
And the eye over-weening into madness.

Turkey-cock, turkey-cock
Are you the bird of the next dawn?

Has the peacock had his day, does he call in vain, screecher,
    for the sun to rise?
The eagle, the dove, and the barnyard rooster, do they call in
    vain, trying to wake the morrow?
And do you await us, wattled father, Westward?
Will your yell do it?

Take up the trail of the vanished American
Where it disappeared at the foot of the crucifix?
Take up the primordial Indian obstinacy,
The more than human, dense insistence of will,
And disdain, and blankness, and onrush, and prise open the
    new day with them?

The East a dead letter, and Europe moribund . . . Is that so?
And those sombre, dead, feather-lustrous Aztecs,
    Amerindians,
In all the sinister splendour of their red blood-sacrifices,
Do they stand under the dawn, half-godly, half-demon,
    awaiting the cry of the turkey-cock?

Or must you go through the fire once more, till you're smelted
    pure,
Slag-wattled turkey-cock,
Dross-jabot?

FIESOLE

BABY TORTOISE

YOU know what it is to be born alone,
Baby tortoise!

The first day to heave your feet little by little from the shell,
Not yet awake,
And remain lapsed on earth,
Not quite alive.

A tiny, fragile, half-animate bean.

To open your tiny beak-mouth, that looks as if it would never
open,
Like some iron door;
To lift the upper hawk-beak from the lower base
And reach your skinny little neck
And take your first bite at some dim bit of herbage,
Alone, small insect,
Tiny bright-eye,
Slow one.

To take your first solitary bite
And move on your slow, solitary hunt.
Your bright, dark little eye,
Your eye of a dark disturbed night,
Under its slow lid, tiny baby tortoise,
So indomitable.

No one ever heard you complain.

You draw your head forward, slowly, from your little wimple
And set forward, slow-dragging, on your four-pinned toes,
Rowing slowly forward.
Whither away, small bird?

Rather like a baby working its limbs,
Except that you make slow, ageless progress
And a baby makes none.

The touch of sun excites you,
And the long ages, and the lingering chill
Make you pause to yawn,
Opening your impervious mouth,
Suddenly beak-shaped, and very wide, like some suddenly
        gaping pincers;
Soft red tongue, and hard thin gums,
Then close the wedge of your little mountain front,
Your face, baby tortoise.

Do you wonder at the world, as slowly you turn your head in
        its wimple
And look with laconic, black eyes?
Or is sleep coming over you again,
The non-life?

You are so hard to wake.

Are you able to wonder?
Or is it just your indomitable will and pride of the first life
Looking round
And slowly pitching itself against the inertia
Which had seemed invincible?

The vast inanimate,
And the fine brilliance of your so tiny eye,
Challenger.

Nay, tiny shell-bird,
What a huge vast inanimate it is, that you must row against,
What an incalculable inertia.

Challenger,
Little Ulysses, fore-runner,
No bigger than my thumb-nail,
Buon viaggio.

All animate creation on your shoulder,
Set forth, little Titan, under your battle-shield.

The ponderous, preponderate,
Inanimate universe;
And you are slowly moving, pioneer, you alone.

How vivid your travelling seems now, in the troubled
        sunshine,
Stoic, Ulyssean atom;
Suddenly hasty, reckless, on high toes.

Voiceless little bird,
Resting your head half out of your wimple
In the slow dignity of your eternal pause.
Alone, with no sense of being alone,
And hence six times more solitary;
Fulfilled of the slow passion of pitching through immemorial
        ages
Your little round house in the midst of chaos.

Over the garden earth,
Small bird,
Over the edge of all things.

Traveller,
With your tail tucked a little on one side
Like a gentleman in a long-skirted coat.

All life carried on your shoulder,
Invincible fore-runner.

THE Cross, the Cross
Goes deeper in than we know,
Deeper into life;
Right into the marrow
And through the bone.

Along the back of the baby tortoise
The scales are locked in an arch like a bridge,
Scale-lapping, like a lobster's sections
Or a bee's.

Then crossways down his sides
Tiger-stripes and wasp-bands.

Five, and five again, and five again,
And round the edges twenty-five little ones,
The sections of the baby tortoise shell.

Four, and a keystone;
Four, and a keystone;
Four, and a keystone;
Then twenty-four, and a tiny little keystone.

It needed Pythagoras to see life playing with counters on the
        living back
Of the baby tortoise;
Life establishing the first eternal mathematical tablet,
Not in stone, like the Judean Lord, or bronze, but in
        life-clouded, life-rosy tortoise shell.

The first little mathematical gentleman
Stepping, wee mite, in his loose trousers
Under all the eternal dome of mathematical law.

Fives, and tens,
Threes and fours and twelves,
All the *volte face* of decimals,
The whirligig of dozens and the pinnacle of seven.

Turn him on his back,
The kicking little beetle,
And there again, on his shell-tender, earth-touching belly,
The long cleavage of division, upright of the eternal cross
And on either side count five,
On each side, two above, on each side, two below
The dark bar horizontal.

The Cross!
It goes right through him, the sprottling insect,
Through his cross-wise cloven psyche,
Through his five-fold complex-nature.

So turn him over on his toes again;
Four pin-point toes, and a problematical thumb-piece,
Four rowing limbs, and one wedge-balancing head,
Four and one makes five, which is the clue to all mathematics.

The Lord wrote it all down on the little slate
Of the baby tortoise.
Outward and visible indication of the plan within,
The complex, manifold involvedness of an individual creature
Plotted out
On this small bird, this rudiment,
This little dome, this pediment
Of all creation,
This slow one.

On he goes, the little one,
Bud of the universe,
Pediment of life.

Setting off somewhere, apparently.
Whither away, brisk egg?

His mother deposited him on the soil as if he were no more
      than droppings,
And now he scuffles tinily past her as if she were an old rusty
      tin.

A mere obstacle,
He veers round the slow great mound of her —
Tortoises always foresee obstacles.

It is no use my saying to him in an emotional voice:
'This is your Mother, she laid you when you were an egg.'

He does not even trouble to answer: 'Woman, what have I to
      do with thee?'
He wearily looks the other way,
And she even more wearily looks another way still,
Each with the utmost apathy,
Incognizant,
Unaware,
Nothing.

As for papa,
He snaps when I offer him his offspring,
Just as he snaps when I poke a bit of stick at him,
Because he is irascible this morning, an irascible tortoise
Being touched with love, and devoid of fatherliness.

Father and mother,
And three little brothers,
And all rambling aimless, like little perambulating pebbles
    scattered in the garden,
Not knowing each other from bits of earth or old tins.

Except that papa and mama are old acquaintances, of course,
Though family feeling there is none, not even the beginnings.

Fatherless, motherless, brotherless, sisterless
Little tortoise.

Row on then, small pebble,
Over the clods of the autumn, wind-chilled sunshine,
Young gaiety.

Does he look for a companion?

No, no, don't think it.
He doesn't know he is alone;
Isolation is his birthright,
This atom.

To row forward, and reach himself tall on spiny toes,
To travel, to burrow into a little loose earth, afraid of the
    night,
To crop a little substance,
To move, and to be quite sure that he is moving:
Basta!
To be a tortoise!
Think of it, in a garden of inert clods
A brisk, brindled little tortoise, all to himself —
Crœsus!

In a garden of pebbles and insects
To roam, and feel the slow heart beat
Tortoise-wise, the first bell sounding
From the warm blood, in the dark-creation morning.

Moving, and being himself,
Slow, and unquestioned,
And inordinately there, O stoic!
Wandering in the slow triumph of his own existence,
Ringing the soundless bell of his presence in chaos,
And biting the frail grass arrogantly,
Decidedly arrogantly.

LUI ET ELLE

SHE is large and matronly
And rather dirty,
A little sardonic-looking, as if domesticity had driven her to it.

Though what she does, except lay four eggs at random in the
      garden once a year
And put up with her husband,
I don't know.

She likes to eat.
She hurries up, striding reared on long uncanny legs,
When food is going.
Oh yes, she can make haste when she likes.

She snaps the soft bread from my hand in great mouthfuls,
Opening her rather pretty wedge of an iron, pristine face
Into an enormously wide-beaked mouth
Like sudden curved scissors,
And gulping at more than she can swallow, and working her
      thick, soft tongue,
And having the bread hanging over her chin.

O Mistress, Mistress,
Reptile mistress,
Your eye is very dark, very bright,
And it never softens
Although you watch.

She knows,
She knows well enough to come for food,
Yet she sees me not;
Her bright eye sees, but not me, not anything,
Sightful, sightless, seeing and visionless,
Reptile mistress.

Taking bread in her curved, gaping, toothless mouth,
She has no qualm when she catches my finger in her steel
      overlapping gums,
But she hangs on, and my shout and my shrinking are nothing
      to her,
She does not even know she is nipping me with her curved
      beak.
Snake-like she draws at my finger, while I drag it in horror
      away.

Mistress, reptile mistress,
You are almost too large, I am almost frightened.

He is much smaller,
Dapper beside her,
And ridiculously small.

Her laconic eye has an earthy, materialistic look,
His, poor darling, is almost fiery.

His wimple, his blunt-prowed face,
His low forehead, his skinny neck, his long, scaled, striving legs,
So striving, striving,
Are all more delicate than she,
And he has a cruel scar on his shell.

Poor darling, biting at her feet,
Running beside her like a dog, biting her earthy, splay feet,
Nipping her ankles,
Which she drags apathetic away, though without retreating
      into her shell.

Agelessly silent,
And with a grim, reptile determination,
Cold, voiceless age-after-age behind him, serpents' long
    obstinacy
Of horizontal persistence.

Little old man
Scuffling beside her, bending down, catching his opportunity,
Parting his steel-trap face, so suddenly, and seizing her scaly
    ankle,
And hanging grimly on,
Letting go at last as she drags away,
And closing his steel-trap face.

His steel-trap, stoic, ageless, handsome face.
Alas, what a fool he looks in this scuffle.

And how he feels it!
The lonely rambler, the stoic, dignified stalker through chaos,
The immune, the animate,
Enveloped in isolation,
Forerunner.
Now look at him!

Alas, the spear is through the side of his isolation.
His adolescence saw him crucified into sex,
Doomed, in the long crucifixion of desire, to seek his
    consummation beyond himself.
Divided into passionate duality,
He, so finished and immune, now broken into desirous
    fragmentariness,
Doomed to make an intolerable fool of himself
In his effort toward completion again.

Poor little earthy house-inhabiting Osiris,
The mysterious bull tore him at adolescence into pieces,
And he must struggle after reconstruction, ignominiously.

And so behold him following the tail
Of that mud-hovel of his slowly rambling spouse,
Like some unhappy bull at the tail of a cow,
But with more than bovine, grim, earth-dank persistence,
Suddenly seizing the ugly ankle as she stretches out to walk,
Roaming over the sods,
Or, if it happen to show, at her pointed, heavy tail
Beneath the low-dropping back-board of her shell.

Their two shells like domed boats bumping,
Hers huge, his small;
Their splay feet rambling and rowing like paddles,
And stumbling mixed up in one another,
In the race of love –
Two tortoises,
She huge, he small.

She seems earthily apathetic,
And he has a reptile's awful persistence.

I heard a woman pitying her, pitying the Mère Tortue.
While I, I pity Monsieur.
'He pesters her and torments her,' said the woman.
How much more is *he* pestered and tormented, say I.

What can he do?
He is dumb, he is visionless,
Conceptionless.
His black, sad-lidded eye sees but beholds not
As her earthen mound moves on,
But he catches the folds of vulnerable, leathery skin,
Nail-studded, that shake beneath her shell,
And drags at these with his beak,
Drags and drags and bites,
While she pulls herself free, and rows her dull mound along.

MAKING his advances
He does not look at her, nor sniff at her,
No, not even sniff at her, his nose is blank.

Only he senses the vulnerable folds of skin
That work beneath her while she sprawls along
In her ungainly pace,
Her folds of skin that work and row
Beneath the earth-soiled hovel in which she moves.

And so he strains beneath her housey walls
And catches her trouser-legs in his beak
Suddenly, or her skinny limb,
And strange and grimly drags at her
Like a dog,
Only agelessly silent, with a reptile's awful persistency.

Grim, gruesome gallantry, to which he is doomed.
Dragged out of an eternity of silent isolation
And doomed to partiality, partial being,
Ache, and want of being,
Want,
Self-exposure, hard humiliation, need to add himself on to her.

Born to walk alone,
Fore-runner,
Now suddenly distracted into this mazy side-track,
This awkward, harrowing pursuit,
This grim necessity from within.

Does she know
As she moves eternally slowly away?
Or is he driven against her with a bang, like a bird flying in the
    dark against a window,
All knowledgeless?

The awful concussion,
And the still more awful need to persist, to follow, follow,
    continue,
Driven, after æons of pristine, fore-god-like singleness and
    oneness,
At the end of some mysterious, red-hot iron,
Driven away from himself into her tracks,
Forced to crash against her.

Stiff, gallant, irascible, crook-legged reptile,
Little gentleman,
Sorry plight,
We ought to look the other way.

Save that, having come with you so far,
We will go on to the end.

TORTOISE SHOUT

I THOUGHT he was dumb,
I said he was dumb,
Yet I've heard him cry.

First faint scream,
Out of life's unfathomable dawn,
Far off, so far, like a madness, under the horizon's dawning rim,
Far, far off, far scream.

Tortoise *in extremis*.

Why were we crucified into sex?
Why were we not left rounded off, and finished in ourselves,
As we began,
As he certainly began, so perfectly alone?

A far, was-it-audible scream,
Or did it sound on the plasm direct?

Worse than the cry of the new-born,
A scream,
A yell,
A shout,
A pæan,
A death-agony,
A birth-cry,
A submission,
All tiny, tiny, far away, reptile under the first dawn.

War-cry, triumph, acute-delight, death-scream reptilian,
Why was the veil torn?
The silken shriek of the soul's torn membrane?
The male soul's membrane
Torn with a shriek half music, half horror.

Crucifixion.
Male tortoise, cleaving behind the hovel-wall of that dense
    female,
Mounted and tense, spread-eagle, out-reaching out of the shell
In tortoise-nakedness,
Long neck, and long vulnerable limbs extruded, spread-eagle
    over her house-roof,
And the deep, secret, all-penetrating tail curved beneath her
    walls,
Reaching and gripping tense, more reaching anguish in
    uttermost tension
Till suddenly, in the spasm of coition, tupping like a jerking
    leap, and oh!
Opening its clenched face from his outstretched neck
And giving that fragile yell, that scream,
Super-audible,
From his pink, cleft, old-man's mouth,
Giving up the ghost,
Or screaming in Pentecost, receiving the ghost.

His scream, and his moment's subsidence,
The moment of eternal silence,

Yet unreleased, and after the moment, the sudden, startling
       jerk of coition, and at once
The inexpressible faint yell –
And so on, till the last plasm of my body was melted back
To the primeval rudiments of life, and the secret.

So he tups, and screams
Time after time that frail, torn scream
After each jerk, the longish interval,
The tortoise eternity,
Agelong, reptilian persistence,
Heart-throb, slow heart-throb, persistent for the next spasm.

I remember, when I was a boy,
I heard the scream of a frog, which was caught with his foot in
       the mouth of an up-starting snake;
I remember when I first heard bull-frogs break into sound in
       the spring;
I remember hearing a wild goose out of the throat of night
Cry loudly, beyond the lake of waters;
I remember the first time, out of a bush in the darkness, a
       nightingale's piercing cries and gurgles startled the depths
       of my soul;
I remember the scream of a rabbit as I went through a wood at
       midnight;
I remember the heifer in her heat, blorting and blorting
       through the hours, persistent and irrepressible;
I remember my first terror hearing the howl of weird, amorous
       cats;
I remember the scream of a terrified, injured horse, the
       sheet-lightning,
And running away from the sound of a woman in labour,
       something like an owl whooing,
And listening inwardly to the first bleat of a lamb,
The first wail of an infant,
And my mother singing to herself,
And the first tenor singing of the passionate throat of a young
       collier, who has long since drunk himself to death,

The first elements of foreign speech
On wild dark lips.

And more than all these,
And less than all these,
This last,
Strange, faint coition yell
Of the male tortoise at extremity,
Tiny from under the very edge of the farthest far-off horizon of
    life.

The cross,
The wheel on which our silence first is broken,
Sex, which breaks up our integrity, our single inviolability, our
    deep silence
Tearing a cry from us.

Sex, which breaks us into voice, sets us calling across the
    deeps, calling, calling for the complement,
Singing, and calling, and singing again, being answered,
    having found.

Torn, to become whole again, after long seeking for what is
    lost,
The same cry from the tortoise as from Christ, the Osiris-cry
    of abandonment,
That which is whole, torn asunder,
That which is in part, finding its whole again throughout the
    universe.

SICILIAN CYCLAMENS

WHEN he pushed his bush of black hair off his brow:
When she lifted her mop from her eyes, and screwed it in a
    knob behind
   — O act of fearful temerity!

When they felt their foreheads bare, naked to heaven, their
    eyes revealed:
When they felt the light of heaven brandished like a knife at
    their defenceless eyes,
And the sea like a blade at their face,
Mediterranean savages:
When they came out, face-revealed, under heaven, from the
    shaggy undergrowth of their own hair
For the first time,
They saw tiny rose cyclamens between their toes, growing
Where the slow toads sat brooding on the past.

Slow toads, and cyclamen leaves
Stickily glistening with eternal shadow
Keeping to earth.
Cyclamen leaves
Toad-filmy, earth-iridescent
Beautiful
Frost-filigreed
Spumed with mud
Snail-nacreous
Low down.

The shaking aspect of the sea
And man's defenceless bare face
And cyclamens putting their ears back.

Long, pensive, slim-muzzled greyhound buds
Dreamy, not yet present,
Drawn out of earth
At his toes.

Dawn-rose
Sub-delighted, stone-engendered
Cyclamens, young cyclamens
Arching
Waking, pricking their ears
Like delicate very-young greyhound bitches

Half-yawning at the open, inexperienced
Vista of day,
Folding back their soundless petalled ears.

Greyhound bitches
Bending their rosy muzzles pensive down,
And breathing soft, unwilling to wake to the new day
Yet sub-delighted.

Ah Mediterranean morning, when our world began!
Far-off Mediterranean mornings,
Pelasgic faces uncovered,
And unbudding cyclamens.

The hare suddenly goes uphill
Laying back her long ears with unwinking bliss.

And up the pallid, sea-blenched Mediterranean stone-slopes
Rose cyclamen, ecstatic fore-runner!
Cyclamens, ruddy-muzzled cyclamens
In little bunches like bunches of wild hares
Muzzles together, ears-aprick
Whispering witchcraft
Like women at a well, the dawn-fountain.

Greece, and the world's morning
Where all the Parthenon marbles still fostered the roots of the
     cyclamen.
Violets
Pagan, rosy-muzzled violets
Autumnal
Dawn-pink,
Dawn-pale
Among squat toad-leaves sprinkling the unborn
Erechtheion marbles.

                                        TAORMINA

BARE ALMOND-TREES

WET almond-trees, in the rain,
Like iron sticking grimly out of earth;
Black almond trunks, in the rain,
Like iron implements twisted, hideous, out of the earth,
Out of the deep, soft fledge of Sicilian winter-green,
Earth-grass uneatable,
Almond trunks curving blackly, iron-dark, climbing the
    slopes.

Almond-tree, beneath the terrace rail,
Black, rusted, iron trunk,
You have welded your thin stems finer,
Like steel, like sensitive steel in the air,
Grey, lavender, sensitive steel, curving thinly and brittly up in
    a parabola.
What are you doing in the December rain?
Have you a strange electric sensitiveness in your steel tips?
Do you feel the air for electric influences
Like some strange magnetic apparatus?
Do you take in messages, in some strange code,
From heaven's wolfish, wandering electricity, that prowls so
    constantly round Etna?
Do you take the whisper of sulphur from the air?
Do you hear the chemical accents of the sun?
Do you telephone the roar of the waters over the earth?
And from all this, do you make calculations?

Sicily, December's Sicily in a mass of rain
With iron branching blackly, rusted like old, twisted
    implements
And brandishing and stooping over earth's wintry fledge,
    climbing the slopes
Of uneatable soft green!

TAORMINA

130

ALMOND BLOSSOM

EVEN iron can put forth,
Even iron.

This is the iron age,
But let us take heart
Seeing iron break and bud,
Seeing rusty iron puff with clouds of blossom.

The almond-tree,
December's bare iron hooks sticking out of earth.

The almond-tree,
That knows the deadliest poison, like a snake
In supreme bitterness.

Upon the iron, and upon the steel,
Odd flakes as if of snow, odd bits of snow,
Odd crumbs of melting snow.

But you mistake, it is not from the sky;
From out the iron, and from out the steel,
Flying not down from heaven, but storming up,
Strange storming up from the dense under-earth
Along the iron, to the living steel
In rose-hot tips, and flakes of rose-pale snow
Setting supreme annunciation to the world.

Nay, what a heart of delicate super-faith,
Iron-breaking,
The rusty swords of almond-trees.

Trees suffer, like races, down the long ages.
They wander and are exiled, they live in exile through long ages
Like drawn blades never sheathed, hacked and gone black
The alien trees in alien lands: and yet
The heart of blossom,
The unquenchable heart of blossom!

Look at the many-cicatrised frail vine, none more scarred and
  frail,
Yet see him fling himself abroad in fresh abandon
From the small wound-stump.

Even the wilful, obstinate, gummy fig-tree
Can be kept down, but he'll burst like a polyp into prolixity.

And the almond-tree, in exile, in the iron age!

This is the ancient southern earth whence the vases were
  baked, amphoras, craters, cantharus, œnochœ, and
  open-hearted cylix,
Bristling now with the iron of almond-trees.

Iron, but unforgotten,
Iron, dawn-hearted,
Ever-beating dawn-heart, enveloped in iron against the exile,
  against the ages.

See it come forth in blossom
From the snow-remembering heart
In long-nighted January,
In the long dark nights of the evening star, and Sirius, and the
  Etna snow-wind through the long night.

Sweating his drops of blood through the long-nighted
  Gethsemane
Into blossom, into pride, into honey-triumph, into most
  exquisite splendour.
Oh, give me the tree of life in blossom
And the Cross sprouting its superb and fearless flowers!

Something must be reassuring to the almond, in the evening
  star, and the snow-wind, and the long, long, nights,
Some memory of far, sun-gentler lands,

So that the faith in his heart smiles again
And his blood ripples with that untellable delight of
　　once-more-vindicated faith,
And the Gethsemane blood at the iron pores unfolds, unfolds,
Pearls itself into tenderness of bud
And in a great and sacred forthcoming steps forth, steps out in
　　one stride
A naked tree of blossom, like a bridegroom bathing in dew,
　　divested of cover,
Frail-naked, utterly uncovered
To the green night-baying of the dog-star, Etna's snow-edged
　　wind
And January's loud-seeming sun.

Think of it, from the iron fastness
Suddenly to dare to come out naked, in perfection of blossom,
　　beyond the sword-rust.
Think, to stand there in full-unfolded nudity, smiling,
With all the snow-wind, and the sun-glare, and the dog-star
　　baying epithalamion.

Oh, honey-bodied beautiful one,
Come forth from iron,
Red your heart is.
Fragile-tender, fragile-tender life-body,
More fearless than iron all the time,
And so much prouder, so disdainful of reluctances.

In the distance like hoar-frost, like silvery ghosts communing
　　on a green hill,
Hoar-frost-like and mysterious.

In the garden raying out
With a body like spray, dawn-tender, and looking about
With such insuperable, subtly-smiling assurance,
Sword-blade-born.

Unpromised,
No bounds being set.
Flaked out and come unpromised,
The tree being life-divine,
Fearing nothing, life-blissful at the core
Within iron and earth.

Knots of pink, fish-silvery
In heaven, in blue, blue heaven,
Soundless, bliss-full, wide-rayed, honey-bodied,
Red at the core,
Red at the core,
Knotted in heaven upon the fine light.

Open,
Open,
Five times wide open,
Six times wide open,
And given, and perfect;
And red at the core with the last sore-heartedness,
Sore-hearted-looking.

                    FONTANA VECCHIA

SNAKE

A SNAKE came to my water-trough
On a hot, hot day, and I in pyjamas for the heat,
To drink there.

In the deep, strange-scented shade of the great dark carob tree
I came down the steps with my pitcher
And must wait, must stand and wait, for there he was at the
      trough before me.

He reached down from a fissure in the earth-wall in the gloom
And trailed his yellow-brown slackness soft-bellied down,
      over the edge of the stone trough
And rested his throat upon the stone bottom,

And where the water had dripped from the tap, in a small
    clearness,
He sipped with his straight mouth,
Softly drank through his straight gums, into his slack long
    body,
Silently.

Someone was before me at my water-trough,
And I, like a second-comer, waiting.

He lifted his head from his drinking, as cattle do,
And looked at me vaguely, as drinking cattle do,
And flickered his two-forked tongue from his lips, and mused
    a moment,
And stooped and drank a little more,
Being earth-brown, earth-golden from the burning bowels of
    the earth
On the day of Sicilian July, with Etna smoking.

The voice of my education said to me
He must be killed,
For in Sicily the black, black snakes are innocent, the gold are
    venomous.

And voices in me said, If you were a man
You would take a stick and break him now, and finish him off.

But must I confess how I liked him,
How glad I was he had come like a guest in quiet, to drink at
    my water-trough
And depart peaceful, pacified, and thankless,
Into the burning bowels of this earth?

Was it cowardice, that I dared not kill him?
Was it perversity, that I longed to talk to him?
Was it humility, to feel so honoured?
I felt so honoured.

And yet those voices:
If you were not afraid, you would kill him!

And truly I was afraid, I was most afraid,
But even so, honoured still more
That he should seek my hospitality
From out the dark door of the secret earth.

He drank enough
And lifted his head, dreamily, as one who has drunken,
And flickered his tongue like a forked night on the air, so
     black,
Seeming to lick his lips,
And looked around like a god, unseeing, into the air,
And slowly turned his head,
And slowly, very slowly, as if thrice adream,
Proceeded to draw his slow length curving round
And climb again the broken bank of my wall-face.

And as he put his head into that dreadful hole,
And as he slowly drew up, snake-easing his shoulders, and
     entered farther,
A sort of horror, a sort of protest against his withdrawing into
     that horrid black hole,
Deliberately going into the blackness, and slowly drawing
     himself after,
Overcame me now his back was turned.

I looked round, I put down my pitcher,
I picked up a clumsy log
And threw it at the water-trough with a clatter.

I think it did not hit him,
But suddenly that part of him that was left behind convulsed in
     undignified haste,
Writhed like lightning, and was gone
Into the black hole, the earth-lipped fissure in the wall-front,
At which, in the intense still noon, I stared with fascination.

And immediately I regretted it.
I thought how paltry, how vulgar, what a mean act!
I despised myself and the voices of my accursed human
    education.

And I thought of the albatross,
And I wished he would come back, my snake.

For he seemed to me again like a king,
Like a king in exile, uncrowned in the underworld,
Now due to be crowned again.

And so, I missed my chance with one of the lords
Of life.
And I have something to expiate:
A pettiness.

TAORMINA

PURPLE ANEMONES

Who gave us flowers?
Heaven? The white God?

Nonsense!
Up out of hell,
From Hades;
Infernal Dis!

Jesus the god of flowers——?
Not he.
Or sun-bright Apollo, him so musical?
Him neither.

Who then?
Say who.
Say it – and it is Pluto,

Dis,
The dark one.
Proserpine's master.

Who contradicts——?

When she broke forth from below,
Flowers came, hell-hounds on her heels.
Dis, the dark, the jealous god, the husband,
Flower-sumptuous-blooded.

Go then, he said.
And in Sicily, on the meadows of Enna,
She thought she had left him;
But opened around her purple anemones,

Caverns,
Little hells of colour, caves of darkness,
Hell, risen in pursuit of her; royal, sumptuous
Pit-falls.

All at her feet
Hell opening;
At her white ankles
Hell rearing its husband-splendid, serpent heads,
Hell-purple, to get at her –
Why did he let her go?
So he could track her down again, white victim.

Ah mastery!
Hell's husband-blossoms
Out on earth again.

Look out, Persephone!
You, Madame Ceres, mind yourself, the enemy is upon you.
About your feet spontaneous aconite,
Hell-glamorous, and purple husband-tyranny
Enveloping your late-enfranchised plains.

You thought your daughter had escaped?
No more stockings to darn for the flower-roots, down in hell?
But ah, my dear!
Aha, the stripe-cheeked whelps, whippet-slim crocuses,
At 'em, boys, at 'em!
Ho, golden-spaniel, sweet alert narcissus,
Smell 'em, smell 'em out!

Those two enfranchised women.

Somebody is coming!
Oho there!

Dark blue anemones!
Hell is up!
Hell on earth, and Dis within the depths!

Run, Persephone, he is after you already.

Why did he let her go?
To track her down;
All the sport of summer and spring, and flowers snapping at
      her ankles and catching her by the hair!
Poor Persephone and her rights for women.

Husband-snared hell-queen,
It is spring.

It is spring,
And pomp of husband-strategy on earth.

Ceres, kiss your girl, you think you've got her back.
The bit of husband-tilth she is,
Persephone!

Poor mothers-in-law!
They are always sold.

It is spring.

TAORMINA

THE ASS

The long-drawn bray of the ass
In the Sicilian twilight —

All mares are dead!
All mares are dead!
Oh-h!
Oh-h-h!
Oh-h-h-h-h — h!!
I can't bear it, I can't bear it,
I can't!
Oh, I can't!
Oh —
There's one left!
There's one left!
One!
There's one . . . left . . .

So ending on a grunt of agonised relief.

This is the authentic Arabic interpretation of the braying of the
 ass.
And Arabs should know.

And yet, as his brass-resonant howling yell resounds through
 the Sicilian twilight
I am not sure —

His big, furry head,
His big, regretful eyes,
His diminished, drooping hindquarters,
His small toes.

Such a dear!
Such an ass!
With such a knot inside him!
He regrets something that he remembers.
That's obvious.

The Steppes of Tartary,
And the wind in his teeth for a bit,
And *noli me tangere*.

Ah then, when he tore the wind with his teeth,
And trod wolves underfoot,
And over-rode his mares as if he were savagely leaping an
        obstacle, to set his teeth in the sun . . .

Somehow, alas, he fell in love,
And was sold into slavery.

He fell into the rut of love,
Poor ass, like man, always in rut,
The pair of them alike in that.

All his soul in his gallant member
And his head gone heavy with the knowledge of desire
And humiliation.

The ass was the first of all animals to fall finally into love,
From obstacle-leaping pride,
Mare obstacle,
Into love, mare-goal, and the knowledge of love.

Hence Jesus rode him in the Triumphant Entry.
Hence his beautiful eyes.
Hence his ponderous head, brooding over desire, and
        downfall, Jesus, and a pack saddle;
Hence he uncovers his big ass-teeth and howls in that agony
        that is half insatiable desire and half unquenchable
        humiliation.
Hence the black cross on his shoulders.

The Arabs were only half right, though they hinted the whole:
Everlasting lament in everlasting desire.

See him standing with his head down, near the Porta
    Cappucini.
Asinello,
Somaro;
With the half-veiled, beautiful eyes, and the pensive face not
    asleep,
Motionless, like a bit of rock.

Has he seen the Gorgon's head, and turned to stone?
Alas, Love did it.
Now he's a jackass, a pack-ass, a donkey, somaro, burro, with
    a boss piling loads on his back.
Tied by the nose at the Porta Cappucini.
And tied in a knot inside, deadlocked between two desires:
To overleap like a male all mares as obstacles
In a leap at the sun;
And to leap in one last heart-bursting leap like a male at the
    goal of a mare,
And there end.
Well, you can't have it both roads.

Hee! Hee! Ehee! Ehow! Ehaw!! Oh! Oh! Oh-h-h!!
The wave of agony bursts in the stone that he was,
Bares his long ass's teeth, flattens his long ass's ears,
    straightens his donkey neck,
And howls his pandemonium on the indignant air.

Yes, it's a quandary.
Jesus rode on him, the first burden on the first beast of burden.
Love on a submissive ass.
So the tale began.

But the ass never forgets.

The horse, being nothing but a nag, will forget.
And men, being mostly geldings and knacker-boned hacks,
    have almost all forgot.
But the ass is a primal creature, and never forgets.

The Steppes of Tartary,
And Jesus on a meek ass-colt: mares: Mary escaping to Egypt:
    Joseph's cudgel.

Hee! Hee! Ehee! Ehow-ow!-ow!-aw!-aw!-aw!
All mares are dead!
Or else I am dead!
One of us, or the pair of us,
I don't know-ow!-ow!
Which!
Not sure-ure-ure
Quite which!
Which!

TAORMINA

FISH

FISH, oh Fish,
So little matters!

Whether the waters rise and cover the earth
Or whether the waters wilt in the hollow places,
All one to you.

Aqueous, subaqueous,
Submerged
And wave-thrilled.

As the waters roll
Roll you.
The waters wash,
You wash in oneness
And never emerge.

Never know,
Never grasp.

Your life a sluice of sensation along your sides,
A flush at the flails of your fins, down the whorl of your tail,
And water wetly on fire in the grates of your gills;
Fixed water-eyes.

Even snakes lie together.

But oh, fish, that rock in water,
You lie only with the waters;
One touch.

No fingers, no hands and feet, no lips;
No tender muzzles,
No wistful bellies,
No loins of desire,
None.

You and the naked element,
Sway-wave.
Curvetting bits of tin in the evening light.

Who is it ejects his sperm to the naked flood?
In the wave-mother?
Who swims enwombed?
Who lies with the waters of his silent passion, womb-element?
— Fish in the waters under the earth.

What price *his* bread upon the waters?

Himself all silvery himself
In the element
No more.

Nothing more.

Himself,
And the element.
Food, of course!

Water-eager eyes,
Mouth-gate open
And strong spine urging, driving;
And desirous belly gulping.

Fear also!
He knows fear!
Water-eyes craning,
A rush that almost screams,
Almost fish-voice
As the pike comes . . .
Then gay fear, that turns the tail sprightly, from a shadow.

Food, and fear, and joie de vivre,
Without love.

The other way about:
Joie de vivre, and fear, and food,
All without love.

Quelle joie de vivre
Dans l'eau!
Slowly to gape through the waters,
Alone with the element;
To sink, and rise, and go to sleep with the waters;
To speak endless inaudible wavelets into the wave;
To breathe from the flood at the gills,
Fish-blood slowly running next to the flood, extracting
        fish-fire;
To have the element under one, like a lover;
And to spring away with a curvetting click in the air,
Provocative.
Dropping back with a slap on the face of the flood.
And merging oneself!

To be a fish!

So utterly without misgiving
To be a fish
In the waters.

Loveless, and so lively!
Born before God was love,
Or life knew loving.
Beautifully beforehand with it all.

Admitted, they swarm in companies,
Fishes.
They drive in shoals.
But soundless, and out of contact.
They exchange no word, no spasm, not even anger.
Not one touch.
Many suspended together, forever apart,
Each one alone with the waters, upon one wave with the rest.

A magnetism in the water between them only.

I saw a water-serpent swim across the Anapo,
And I said to my heart, *look, look at him!*
With his head up, steering like a bird!
He's a rare one, but he belongs . . .

But sitting in a boat on the Zeller lake
And watching the fishes in the breathing waters
Lift and swim and go their way –

I said to my heart, *who are these?*
And my heart couldn't own them . . .

A slim young pike, with smart fins
And grey-striped suit, a young cub of a pike
Slouching along away below, half out of sight,
Like a lout on an obscure pavement . . .

Aha, there's somebody in the know!

But watching closer
That motionless deadly motion,
That unnatural barrel body, that long ghoul nose, . . .
I left off hailing him.

I had made a mistake, I didn't know him,
This grey, monotonous soul in the water,
This intense individual in shadow,
Fish-alive.

I didn't know his God,
I didn't know his God.

Which is perhaps the last admission that life has to wring out
        of us.

I saw, dimly,
Once a big pike rush,
And small fish fly like splinters.
And I said to my heart, *there are limits
To you, my heart;
And to the one God.
Fish are beyond me.*

Other Gods
Beyond my range . . . gods beyond my God . . .

They are beyond me, are fishes.
I stand at the pale of my being
And look beyond, and see
Fish, in the outerwards,
As one stands on a bank and looks in.

I have waited with a long rod
And suddenly pulled a gold-and-greenish, lucent fish from
        below,
And had him fly like a halo round my head,
Lunging in the air on the line.

Unhooked his gorping, water-horny mouth,
And seen his horror-tilted eye,
His red-gold, water-precious, mirror-flat bright eye;
And felt him beat in my hand, with his mucous, leaping
      life-throb.

And my heart accused itself
Thinking: *I am not the measure of creation.*
This is beyond me, this fish.
His God stands outside my God.

And the gold-and-green pure lacquer-mucous comes off in my
      hand,
And the red-gold mirror-eye stares and dies,
And the water-suave contour dims.

But not before I have had to know
He was born in front of my sunrise,
Before my day.

He outstarts me.
And I, a many-fingered horror of daylight to him,
Have made him die.

Fishes,
With their gold, red eyes, and green-pure gleam, and
      under-gold,
And their pre-world loneliness,
And more-than-lovelessness,
And white meat;
They move in other circles.

Outsiders.
Water-wayfarers.
Things of one element.
Aqueous,
Each by itself.

Cats, and the Neapolitans,
Sulphur sun-beasts,
Thirst for fish as for more-than-water;
Water-alive
To quench their over-sulphureous lusts.

But I, I only wonder
And don't know.
I don't know fishes.

In the beginning
Jesus was called The Fish. . .
And in the end.

ZELL-AM-SEE

MAN AND BAT

WHEN I went into my room, at mid-morning,
Say ten o'clock . . .
My room, a crash-box over that great stone rattle
The Via de' Bardi . . .

When I went into my room at mid-morning
Why? . . . a bird!

A bird
Flying round the room in insane circles.

In insane circles!
. . . *A bat!*

A disgusting bat
At mid-morning! . . .

Out! Go out!

Round and round and round
With a twitchy, nervous, intolerable flight,
And a neurasthenic lunge,
And an impure frenzy;
A bat, big as a swallow!

Out, out of my room!

The venetian shutters I push wide
To the free, calm upper air;
Loop back the curtains . . .

Now out, out from my room!

So to drive him out, flicking with my white handkerchief: *Go!*
But he will not.

Round and round and round
In an impure haste,
Fumbling, a beast in air,
And stumbling, lunging and touching the walls, the bell-wires
About my room!

Always refusing to go out into the air
Above that crash-gulf of the Via de' Bardi,
Yet blind with frenzy, with cluttered fear.

At last he swerved into the window bay,
But blew back, as if an incoming wind blew him in again.
A strong inrushing wind.

And round and round and round!
Blundering more insane, and leaping, in throbs, to clutch at a
    corner,
At a wire, at a bell-rope:
On and on, watched relentless by me, round and round in my
    room,

Round and round and dithering with tiredness and haste and
    increasing delirium
Flicker-splashing round my room.

I would not let him rest;
Not one instant cleave, cling like a blot with his breast to the
    wall
In an obscure corner.
Not an instant!

I flicked him on,
Trying to drive him through the window.

Again he swerved into the window bay
And I ran forward, to frighten him forth.
But he rose, and from a terror worse than me he flew past me
Back into my room, and round, round, round in my room
Clutch, cleave, stagger,
Dropping about the air
Getting tired.

Something seemed to blow him back from the window
Every time he swerved at it;
Back on a strange parabola, then round, round, dizzy in my
    room.

He *could* not go out;
I also realised . . .

It was the light of day which he could not enter,
Any more than I could enter the white-hot door of a
    blast-furnace.
He could not plunge into the daylight that streamed at the
    window.
It was asking too much of his nature.

Worse even than the hideous terror of me with my
    handkerchief
Saying: *Out, go out!* . . .
Was the horror of white daylight in the window!

So I switched on the electric light, thinking: *Now*
The outside will seem brown . . .

But no.
The outside did not seem brown.
And he did not mind the yellow electric light.

Silent!
He was having a silent rest.
But never!
Not in my room.

Round and round and round
Near the ceiling as if in a web
Staggering;
Plunging, falling out of the web,
Broken in heaviness,
Lunging blindly,
Heavier;
And clutching, clutching for one second's pause,
Always, as if for one drop of rest,
One little drop.

And I!
Never, I say . . .
Go out!

Flying slower,
Seeming to stumble, to fall in air.
Blind-weary.

Yet never able to pass the whiteness of light into freedom . . .
A bird would have dashed through, come what might.

152

Fall, sink, lurch, and round and round
Flicker, flicker-heavy;
Even wings heavy:
And cleave in a high corner for a second, like a clot, also a
    prayer.

But no.
Out, you beast.

Till he fell in a corner, palpitating, spent.
And there, a clot, he squatted and looked at me.
With sticking-out, bead-berry eyes, black,
And improper derisive ears,
And shut wings,
And brown, furry body.

Brown, nut-brown, fine fur!
But it might as well have been hair on a spider; thing
With long, black-paper ears.

So, a dilemma!
He squatted there like something unclean.

No, he must not squat, nor hang, obscene, in my room!

Yet nothing on earth will give him courage to pass the sweet
    fire of day.

What then?
Hit him and kill him and throw him away?

Nay,
I didn't create him.
Let the God that created him be responsible for his death . . .
Only, in the bright day, I will not have this clot in my room.

Let the God who is maker of bats watch with them in their
    unclean corners . . .

I admit a God in every crevice,
But not bats in my room;
Nor the God of bats, while the sun shines.

So out, out you brute! . . .
And he lunged, flight-heavy, away from me, sideways, *a
    sghembo!*
And round and round and round my room, a clot with wings
Impure even in weariness.

Wings dark skinny and flapping the air,
Lost their flicker.
Spent.

He fell again with a little thud
Near the curtain on the floor.
And there lay.

Ah, death, death,
You are no solution!
Bats must be bats.

Only life has a way out.
And the human soul is fated to wide-eyed responsibility
In life.

So I picked him up in a flannel jacket,
Well covered, lest he should bite me.
For I would have had to kill him if he'd bitten me, the impure
    one . . .
And he hardly stirred in my hand, muffled up.

Hastily, I shook him out of the window.

And away he went!
Fear craven in his tail.
Great haste, and straight, almost bird straight above the Via
    de' Bardi.

Above that crash-gulf of exploding whips,
Towards the Borgo San Jacopo.

And now, at evening, as he flickers over the river
Dipping with petty triumphant flight, and tittering over the
    sun's departure,
I believe he chirps, pipistrello, seeing me here on this terrace
    writing:
There he sits, the long loud one!
But I am greater than he . . .
I escaped him . . .

FLORENCE

HE-GOAT

SEE his black nose snubbed back, pressed over like a whale's
    blow-holes,
As if his nostrils were going to curve back to the root of his
    tail.

As he charges slow among the herd
And rows among the females like a ship pertinaciously,
Heavy with a rancid cargo, through the lesser ships —
Old father
Sniffing forever ahead of him, at the rear of the goats, that they
    lift the little door;
And rowing on, unarrived, no matter how often he enter:
Like a big ship pushing her bow-sprit over the little ships
Then swerving and steering afresh
And never, never arriving at journey's end, at the rear of the
    female ships.

Yellow eyes incomprehensible with thin slits
To round-eyed us.

Yet if you had whorled horns of bronze in a frontal dark wall
At the end of a back-bone ridge, like a straight sierra roqueña,

And nerves urging forward to the wall, you'd have eyes like
    his,
Especially if, being given a needle's eye of egress elsewhere
You tried to look back to it, and couldn't.

Sometimes he turns with a start, to fight, to challenge, to
    suddenly butt.
And then you see the God that he is, in a cloud of black hair
And storm-lightning-slitted eye.
Splendidly planting his feet, one rocky foot striking the ground
    with a sudden rock-hammer announcement:

I am here!
And suddenly lowering his head, the whorls of bone and of
    horn
Slowly revolving towards unexploded explosion,
As from the stem of his bristling, lightning-conductor tail
In a rush up the shrieking duct of his vertebral way
Runs a rage drawn in from the ether divinely through him
Towards a shock and a crash and a smiting of horns ahead.

That is a grand old lust of his, to gather the great
Rage of the sullen-stagnating atmosphere of goats
And bring it hurtling to a head, with crash of horns against the
    horns
Of the opposite enemy goat,
Thus hammering the mettle of goats into proof, and smiting
    out
The godhead of goats from the shock.
Things of iron are beaten on the anvil,
And he-goat is anvil to he-goat, and hammer to he-goat
In the business of beating the mettle of goats to a god-head.

But they've taken his enemy from him
And left him only his libidinousness,
His nostrils turning back, to sniff at even himself
And his slitted eyes seeking the needle's eye,
His own, unthreaded, forever.

So it is, when they take the enemy from us,
And we can't fight.

He is not fatherly, like the bull, massive Providence of hot
    blood;
The goat is an egoist, aware of himself, devilish aware of
    himself,
And full of malice prepense, and overweening, determined to
    stand on the highest peak
Like the devil, and look on the world as his own.

And as for love:
With a needle of long red flint he stabs in the dark
At the living rock he is up against;
While she with her goaty mouth stands smiling the while as he
    strikes, since sure
He will never *quite* strike home, on the target-quick, for her
    quick
Is just beyond the range of the arrow he shoots
From his leap at the zenith in her, so it falls just short of the
    mark, far enough.
It is over before it is finished.
She, smiling with goaty munch-mouth, Mona Lisa, arranges it
    so.

Orgasm after orgasm after orgasm
And he smells so rank, and his nose goes back,
And never an enemy brow-metalled to thresh it out with in the
    open field;
Never a mountain peak, to be king of the castle.
Only those eternal females to overleap and surpass, and never
    succeed.

The involved voluptuousness of the soft-footed cat
Who is like a fur folding a fur,
The cat who laps blood, and knows
The soft welling of blood invincible even beyond bone or
    metal of bone.

157

The soft, the secret, the unfathomable blood
The cat has lapped
And known it subtler than frisson-shaken nerves,
Stronger than multiplicity of bone on bone
And darker than even the arrows of violentest will
Can pierce, for that is where will gives out, like a sinking stone
     that can sink no further.

But he-goat,
Black procreant male of the selfish will and libidinous desire,
God in black cloud with curving horns of bronze,
Find an enemy, Egoist, and clash the cymbals in face-to-face
     defiance,
And let the lightning out of your smothered dusk.

Forget the female herd for a bit,
And fight to be boss of the world.
Fight, old Satan with a selfish will, fight for your selfish will;
Fight to be the devil on the tip of the peak
Overlooking the world for his own.

But bah, how can he, poor domesticated beast!

                                 TAORMINA

ELEPHANT

You go down shade to the river, where naked men sit on flat
     brown rocks, to watch the ferry, in the sun;
And you cross the ferry with the naked people, go up the
     tropical lane
Through the palm-trees and past hollow paddy-fields where
     naked men are threshing rice
And the monolithic water-buffaloes, like old, muddy stones
     with hair on them, are being idle;
And through the shadow of bread-fruit trees, with their dark
     green, glossy, fanged leaves
Very handsome, and some pure yellow fanged leaves;

Out into the open, where the path runs on the top of a dyke
    between paddy-fields:
And there, of course, you meet a huge and mud-grey elephant
    advancing his frontal bone, his trunk curled round a log
    of wood:
So you step down the bank, to make way.

Shuffle, shuffle, and his little wicked eye has seen you as he
    advances above you,
The slow beast curiously spreading his round feet for the dust.
And the slim naked man slips down, and the beast deposits the
    lump of wood, carefully.
The keeper hooks the vast knee, the creature salaams.

White man, you are saluted.
Pay a few cents.

But the best is the Pera-hera, at midnight, under the tropical
    stars,
With a pale little wisp of a Prince of Wales, diffident, up in a
    small pagoda on the temple side
And white people in evening dress buzzing and crowding the
    stand upon the grass below and opposite:
And at last the Pera-hera procession, flambeaux aloft in the
    tropical night, of blazing cocoa-nut,
Naked dark men beneath,
And the huge frontal of three great elephants stepping forth to
    the tom-tom's beat, in the torch-light,
Slowly sailing in gorgeous apparel through the flame-light, in
    front of a towering, grimacing white image of wood.

The elephant bells striking slow, tong-tong, tong-tong,
To music and queer chanting:
Enormous shadow-processions filing on in the flare of fire
In the fume of cocoa-nut oil, in the sweating tropical night,
In the noise of the tom-toms and singers;

Elephants after elephants curl their trunks, vast shadows, and
    some cry out
As they approach and salaam, under the dripping fire of the
    torches
That pale fragment of a Prince up there, whose motto is *Ich
dien*.

Pale, dispirited Prince, with his chin on his hands, his nerves
    tired out,
Watching and hardly seeing the trunk-curl approach and
    clumsy, knee-lifting salaam
Of the hugest, oldest of beasts, in the night and the fire-flare
    below.

He is royalty, pale and dejected fragment up aloft.
And down below huge homage of shadowy beasts, barefoot
    and trunk-lipped in the night.

Chieftains, three of them abreast, on foot
Strut like peg-tops, wound around with hundreds of yards of
    fine linen.
They glimmer with tissue of gold, and golden threads on a
    jacket of velvet,
And their faces are dark, and fat, and important.

They are royalty, dark-faced royalty, showing the conscious
    whites of their eyes
And stepping in homage, stubborn, to that nervous pale lad up
    there.

More elephants, tong, tong-tong, loom up,
Huge, more tassels swinging, more dripping fire of new
    cocoa-nut cressets
High, high flambeaux, smoking of the east;
And scarlet hot embers of torches knocked out of the sockets
    among bare feet of elephants and men on the path in the
    dark.

And devil dancers, luminous with sweat, dancing on to the
    shudder of drums,
Tom-toms, weird music of the devil, voices of men from the
    jungle singing;
Endless, under the Prince.

Towards the tail of the everlasting procession
In the long hot night, more dancers from insignificant villages,
And smaller, more frightened elephants.
Men-peasants from jungle villages dancing and running with
    sweat and laughing,
Naked dark men with ornaments on, on their naked arms and
    their naked breasts, the grooved loins
Gleaming like metal with running sweat as they suddenly turn,
    feet apart,
And dance and dance, forever dance, with breath half sobbing
    in dark, sweat-shining breasts,
And lustrous great tropical eyes unveiled now, gleaming a kind
    of laugh,
A naked, gleaming dark laugh, like a secret out in the dark,
And flare of a tropical energy, tireless, afire in the dark, slim
    limbs and breasts;
Perpetual, fire-laughing motion, among the slow shuffle
Of elephants,
The hot dark blood of itself a-laughing, wet, half-devilish, men
    all motion
Approaching under that small pavilion, and tropical eyes
    dilated look up
Inevitably look up
To the Prince,
To that tired remnant of royalty up there
Whose motto is *Ich dien*.

As if the homage of the kindled blood of the east
Went up in wavelets to him, from the breasts and eyes of
    jungle torch-men.
And he couldn't take it.

What would they do, those jungle men running with sweat,
    with the strange dark laugh in their eyes, glancing up,
And the sparse-haired elephants slowly following,
If they knew that his motto was *Ich dien?*
And that he meant it.

They begin to understand,
The rickshaw boys begin to understand;
And then the devil comes into their faces,
But a different sort, a cold, rebellious, jeering devil.

In elephants and the east are two devils, in all men maybe.
The mystery of the dark mountain of blood, reeking in
    homage, in lust, in rage,
And passive with everlasting patience;
Then the little, cunning pig-devil of the elephant's lurking eyes,
    the unbeliever.

We dodged, when the Pera-hera was finished, under the
    hanging, hairy pig's tails
And the flat, flaccid mountains of the elephants' standing
    haunches,
Vast-blooded beasts,
Myself so little dodging rather scared against the eternal
    wrinkled pillars of their legs, as they were being
    dismantled;
Then I knew they were dejected, having come to hear the
    repeated
Royal summons: *Dient Ihr!*
Serve!
*Serve, vast mountainous blood, in submission and splendour,
    serve royalty.*
Instead of which, the silent, fatal emission from that pale
    shattered boy up there:
Ich dien.

That's why the night fell in frustration.

That's why, as the elephants ponderously, with unseeming
   swiftness galloped uphill in the night, going back to the
   jungle villages,

As the elephant bells sounded tong-tong-tong, bell of the
   temple of blood, in the night, swift-striking,

And the crowd like a field of rice in the dark gave way like
   liquid to the dark

Looming gallop of the beasts,

It was as if the great bare bulks of elephants in the obscure
   light went over the hill-brow swiftly, with their tails
   between their legs, in haste to get away,

Their bells sounding frustrate and sinister.

And all the dark-faced, cotton-wrapped people, more
   numerous and whispering than grains of rice in a rice-field
   at night,

All the dark-faced, cotton-wrapped people, a countless host on
   the shores of the lake, like thick wild rice by the water's
   edge,

Waiting for the fireworks of the after-show,

As the rockets went up, and the glare passed over countless
   faces, dark as black rice growing,

Showing a glint of teeth, and glancing tropical eyes aroused in
   the night,

There was the faintest twist of mockery in every face, across
   the hiss of wonders as the rocket burst

High, high up, in flakes, shimmering flakes of blue fire, above
   the palm trees of the islet in the lake,

O faces upturned to the glare, O tropical wonder, wonder, a
   miracle in heaven!

And the shadow of a jeer, of underneath disappointment, as
   the rocket-coruscation died, and shadow was the same as
   before.

They were foiled, the myriad whispering dark-faced
   cotton-wrapped people.

They had come to see royalty,

To bow before royalty, in the land of elephants, bow deep,
 bow deep.
Bow deep, for it's good as a draught of cool water to bow very,
 very low to the royal.

And all there was to bow to, a weary, diffident boy whose
 motto is *Ich dien.*
I serve! I serve! in all the weary irony of his mien — *'Tis I who
 serve!*
Drudge to the public.

I wish they had given the three feathers to me;
That I had been he in the pavilion, as in a pepper-box aloft and
 alone
To stand and hold feathers, three feathers above the world,
And to say to them: *Dient Ihr! Dient!*
Omnes, vos omnes, servite.
Serve me, I am meet to be served.
Being royal of the gods.

And to the elephants:
First great beasts of the earth
A prince has come back to you,
Blood-mountains.
Crook the knee and be glad.

KANDY

KANGAROO

IN the northern hemisphere
Life seems to leap at the air, or skim under the wind
Like stags on rocky ground, or pawing horses, or springy
 scut-tailed rabbits.

Or else rush horizontal to charge at the sky's horizon,
Like bulls or bisons or wild pigs.

Or slip like water slippery towards its ends,
As foxes, stoats, and wolves, and prairie dogs.

Only mice, and moles, and rats, and badgers, and beavers, and
    perhaps bears
Seem belly-plumbed to the earth's mid-navel.
Or frogs that when they leap come flop, and flop to the centre
    of the earth.

But the yellow antipodal Kangaroo, when she sits up
Who can unseat her, like a liquid drop that is heavy, and just
    touches earth.

The downward drip.
The down-urge.
So much denser than cold-blooded frogs.

Delicate mother Kangaroo
Sitting up there rabbit-wise, but huge, plumb-weighted,
And lifting her beautiful slender face, oh! so much more gently
    and finely-lined than a rabbit's, or than a hare's,
Lifting her face to nibble at a round white peppermint drop,
    which she loves, sensitive mother Kangaroo.

Her sensitive, long, pure-bred face.
Her full antipodal eyes, so dark,
So big and quiet and remote, having watched so many empty
    dawns in silent Australia.

Her little loose hands, and drooping Victorian shoulders.
And then her great weight below the waist, her vast pale belly
With a thin young yellow little paw hanging out, and straggle
    of a long thin ear, like ribbon,
Like a funny trimming to the middle of her belly, thin little
    dangle of an immature paw, and one thin ear.

Her belly, her big haunches
And in addition, the great muscular python-stretch of her tail.

There, she shan't have any more peppermint drops.
So she wistfully, sensitively sniffs the air, and then turns, goes
    off in slow sad leaps
On the long flat skis of her legs,
Steered and propelled by that steel-strong snake of a tail.

Stops again, half turns, inquisitive to look back.
While something stirs quickly in her belly, and a lean little face
    comes out, as from a window,
Peaked and a bit dismayed,
Only to disappear again quickly away from the sight of the
    world, to snuggle down in the warmth,
Leaving the trail of a different paw hanging out.

Still she watches with eternal, cocked wistfulness!
How full her eyes are, like the full, fathomless, shining eyes of
    an Australian black-boy
Who has been lost so many centuries on the margins of
    existence!

She watches with insatiable wistfulness.
Untold centuries of watching for something to come,
For a new signal from life, in that silent lost land of the South.

Where nothing bites but insects and snakes and the sun, small
    life.
Where no bull roared, no cow ever lowed, no stag cried, no
    leopard screeched, no lion coughed, no dog barked,
But all was silent save for parrots occasionally, in the haunted
    blue bush.

Wistfully watching, with wonderful liquid eyes.
And all her weight, all her blood, dripping sack-wise down
    towards the earth's centre,
And the live little one taking in its paw at the door of her belly.

Leap then, and come down on the line that draws to the
    earth's deep, heavy centre.

SYDNEY

EAGLE IN NEW MEXICO

TOWARDS the sun, towards the south-west
A scorched breast.
A scorched breast, breasting the sun like an answer,
Like a retort.
An eagle at the top of a low cedar-bush
On the sage-ash desert
Reflecting the scorch of the sun from his breast;
Eagle, with the sickle dripping darkly above.

Erect, scorched-pallid out of the hair of the cedar,
Erect, with the god-thrust entering him from below,
Eagle gloved in feathers
In scorched white feathers
In burnt dark feathers
In feathers still fire-rusted;
Sickle-overswept, sickle dripping over and above.

Sun-breaster,
Staring two ways at once, to right and left;
Masked-one
Dark-visaged
Sickle-masked
With iron between your two eyes;
You feather-gloved
To the feet;
Foot-fierce;
Erect one;
The god-thrust entering you steadily from below.

You never look at the sun with your two eyes.
Only the inner eye of your scorched broad breast
Looks straight at the sun.

You are dark
Except scorch-pale-breasted;
And dark cleaves down and weapon-hard downward curving
At your scorched breast,
Like a sword of Damocles,
Beaked eagle.

You've dipped it in blood so many times
That dark face-weapon, to temper it well,
Blood-thirsty bird.
Why do you front the sun so obstinately,
American eagle?
As if you owed him an old, old grudge, great sun: or an old,
        old allegiance.

When you pick the red smoky heart from a rabbit or a
        light-blooded bird
Do you lift it to the sun, as the Aztec priests used to lift red
        hearts of men?

Does the sun need steam of blood do you think
In America, still,
Old eagle?

Does the sun in New Mexico sail like a fiery bird of prey in the
        sky
Hovering?

Does he shriek for blood?
Does he fan great wings above the prairie, like a hovering,
        blood-thirsty bird?

And are you his priest, big eagle
Whom the Indians aspire to?
Is there a bond of bloodshed between you?

Is your continent cold from the ice-age still, that the sun is so
    angry?
Is the blood of your continent somewhat reptilian still,
That the sun should be greedy for it?

I don't yield to you, big, jowl-faced eagle.
Nor you nor your blood-thirsty sun
That sucks up blood
Leaving a nervous people.

Fly off, big bird with a big black back.
Fly slowly away, with a rust of fire in your tail,
Dark as you are on your dark side, eagle of heaven.

Even the sun in heaven can be curbed and chastened at last
By the life in the hearts of men.
And you, great bird, sun-starer, heavy black beak
Can be put out of office as sacrifice bringer.

                              TAOS

AUTUMN AT TAOS

OVER the rounded sides of the Rockies, the aspens of autumn,
The aspens of autumn,
Like yellow hair of a tigress brindled with pines.

Down on my hearth-rug of desert, sage of the mesa,
An ash-grey pelt
Of wolf all hairy and level, a wolf's wild pelt.
Trot-trot to the mottled foot-hills, cedar-mottled and piñon;
Did you ever see an otter?
Silvery-sided, fish-fanged, fierce-faced, whiskered, mottled.

When I trot my little pony through the aspen-trees of the
    canyon,
Behold me trotting at ease betwixt the slopes of the golden
Great and glistening-feathered legs of the hawk of Horus;
The golden hawk of Horus
Astride above me.

But under the pines
I go slowly
As under the hairy belly of a great black bear.

Glad to emerge and look back
On the yellow, pointed aspen-trees laid one on another like
    feathers,
Feather over feather on the breast of the great and golden
Hawk as I say of Horus.

Pleased to be out in the sage and the pine fish-dotted foothills,
Past the otter's whiskers,
On to the fur of the wolf-pelt that strews the plain.

And then to look back to the rounded sides of the squatting
    Rockies.
Tigress brindled with aspen,
Jaguar-splashed, puma-yellow, leopard-livid slopes of
    America.

Make big eyes, little pony,
At all these skins of wild beasts;
They won't hurt you.

Fangs and claws and talons and beaks and hawk-eyes
Are nerveless just now.
So be easy.

TAOS

THE RED WOLF

OVER the heart of the west, the Taos desert
Circles an eagle,
And it's dark between me and him.

The sun, as he waits a moment, huge and liquid
Standing without feet on the rim of the far-off mesa
Says: *Look for a last long time then! Look! Look well! I am
    going.*
So he pauses and is beholden, and straightway is gone.

And the Indian, in a white sheet
Wrapped to the eyes, the sheet bound close on his brows,
Stands saying: *See, I'm invisible!*
Behold how you can't behold me!
The invisible in its shroud!

Now that the sun has gone, and the aspen leaves
And the cotton-wood leaves are fallen, as good as fallen,
And the ponies are in corral,
And it's night:
Why, more has gone than all these;
And something has come.
A red wolf stands on the shadow's dark red rim.

Day has gone to dust on the sage-grey desert
Like a white Christus fallen to dust from a cross;
To dust, to ash, on the twilit floor of the desert.
And a black crucifix like a dead tree spreading wings;
Maybe a black eagle with its wings out
Left lonely in the night
In a sort of worship.

And coming down upon us, out of the dark concave
Of the eagle's wings,
And the coffin-like slit where the Indian's eyes are,
And the absence of cotton-wood leaves, or of aspen,

Even the absence of dark-crossed donkeys:
Come tall old demons, smiling
The Indian smile,
Saying: *How do you do, you pale-face?*

I am very well, old demon.
How are you?

Call me Harry if you will,
Call me Old Harry, says he.
Or the abbreviation of Nicolas,
Nick, Old Nick, maybe.

Well, you're a dark old demon,
And I'm a pale-face like a homeless dog
That has followed the sun from the dawn through the east
Trotting east and east and east till the sun himself went home,
And left me homeless here in the dark at your door.
How do you think we'll get on,
Old demon, you and I?

You and I, you pale-face,
Pale-face you and I
Don't get on.

Mightn't we try?

Where's your God, you white one?
Where's your white God?

He fell to dust as the twilight fell,
Was fume as I trod
The last step out of the east.

Then you're a lost white dog of a pale-face,
And the day's now dead . . .

Touch me carefully, old father,
My beard is red.

Thin red wolf of a pale-face,
Thin red wolf, go home.

I have no home, old father.
That's why I come.

We take no hungry stray from the pale-face . . .

Father, you are not asked.
I am come. I am here. The red-dawn-wolf
Sniffs round your place.
Lifts up his voice and howls to the walls of the pueblo,
Announcing he's here.

The dogs of the dark pueblo
Have long fangs . . .

Has the red wolf trotted east and east and east,
From the far, far other end of the day
To fear a few fangs?

Across the pueblo river
That dark old demon and I
Thus say a few words to each other.

And wolf, he calls me, and red.
I call him no names.
He says, however, he is Star-Road.
I say, he can go back the same gait.

As for me . . .
Since I trotted at the tail of the sun as far as ever the creature
        went west,
And lost him here,

I'm going to sit down on my tail right here
And wait for him to come back with a new story.
I'm the red wolf, says the dark old father.
All right, the red dawn wolf I am.

TAOS

BIBBLES

BIBBLES
Little black dog in New Mexico,
Little black snub-nosed bitch with a shoved-out jaw
And a wrinkled reproachful look;
Little black female pup, sort of French bull, they say,
With bits of brindle coming through, like rust, to show you're
    not pure;
Not pure, Bibbles,
Bubsey, bat-eared dog;
Not black enough!

First live thing I've 'owned' since the lop-eared rabbits when I
    was a lad,
And those over-prolific white mice, and Adolf, and Rex whom
    I didn't own.
And even now, Bibbles, little Ma'am, it's you who
    appropriated me, not I you.
As Benjamin Franklin appropriated Providence to his
    purposes.

Oh Bibbles, black little bitch
I'd never have let you appropriate me, had I known.
I never dreamed, till now, of the awful time the Lord must
    have, 'owning' humanity,
Especially democratic live-by-love humanity.

Oh Bibbles, oh Pips, oh Pipsey
You little black love-bird!
Don't you love *everybody*!!!

174

Just everybody.
You love 'em all.
Believe in the One Identity, don't you,
You little Walt-Whitmanesque bitch?

First time I lost you in Taos plaza
And found you after endless chasing,
Came upon you prancing round the corner in exuberant,
        bibbling affection
After the black-green skirts of a yellow-green old Mexican
        woman
Who hated you, and kept looking round at you and cursing
        you in a mutter,
While you pranced and bounced with love of her, you
        indiscriminating animal,
All your wrinkled *miserere* Chinese black little face beaming
And your black little body bouncing and wriggling
With indiscriminate love, Bibbles;
I had a moment's pure detestation of you.
As I rushed like an idiot round the corner after you
Yelling: *Pips! Pips! Bibbles!*

I've had moments of hatred of you since,
Loving everybody!
'To you, whoever you are, with endless embrace!' –
That's you, Pipsey,
With your imbecile bit of a tail in a love-flutter.
You omnipip.

Not that you're merely a softy, oh dear me no,
You know which side your bread is buttered.
You don't care a rap for anybody.
But you love lying warm between warm human thighs,
        indiscriminate,
And you love to make somebody love you, indiscriminate,
You love to lap up affection, to wallow in it,
And then turn tail to the next comer, for a new dollop.

And start prancing and licking and cuddling again,
    indiscriminate.

Oh yes, I know your little game.

Yet you're so nice,
So quick, like a little black dragon.
So fierce, when the coyotes howl, barking back like a whole
    little lion, and rumbling,
And starting forward in the dusk, with your little black fur all
    bristling like plush
Against those coyotes, who would swallow you like an oyster.

And in the morning, when the bedroom door is opened,
Rushing in like a little black whirlwind, leaping straight as an
    arrow on the bed at the pillow
And turning the day suddenly into a black tornado of *joie de
    vivre*, Chinese dragon.

So funny
Lobbing wildly through deep snow like a rabbit,
Hurtling like a black ball through the snow,
Champing it, tossing a mouthful,
Little black spot in the landscape!

So absurd
Pelting behind on the dusty trail when the horse sets off home
    at a gallop:
Left in the dust behind like a dust-ball tearing along
Coming up on fierce little legs, tearing fast to catch up, a real
    little dust-pig, ears almost blown away,
And black eyes bulging bright in a dust-mask
Chinese-dragon-wrinkled, with a pink mouth grinning, under
    jaw shoved out
And white teeth showing in your dragon-grin as you race, you
    split-face,
Like a trundling projectile swiftly whirling up,

Cocking your eyes at me as you come alongside, to see if I'm I
    on the horse,
And panting with that split grin,
All your game little body dust-smooth like a little pig, poor
    Pips.

Plenty of game old spirit in you, Bibbles.
Plenty of game old spunk, little bitch.

How you hate being brushed with the boot-brush, to brush all
    that dust out of your wrinkled face,
Don't you?
How you hate being made to look undignified, Ma'am;
How you hate being laughed at, Miss Superb!

Blackberry face!

Plenty of conceit in you.
Unblemished belief in your own perfection
And utter lovableness, you ugly-mug;
Chinese puzzle-face,
Wrinkled underhung physog that looks as if it had done with
    everything,
Through with everything.

Instead of which you sit there and roll your head like a canary
And show a tiny bunch of white teeth in your underhung
    blackness,
Self-conscious little bitch,
Aiming again at being loved.

Let the merest scallywag come to the door and you leap your
    very dearest love at him,
As if now, at last, here was the one you *finally* loved,
Finally loved;
And even the dirtiest scallywag is taken in,
Thinking: *This dog sure has taken a fancy to me.*

You miserable little bitch of love-tricks,
I know your game.

Me or the Mexican who comes to chop wood
All the same,
All humanity is jam to you.

Everybody so dear, and yourself so ultra-beloved
That you have to run out at last and eat filth,
Gobble up filth, you horror, swallow utter abomination and
    fresh-dropped dung.

You stinker.
You worse than a carrion-crow.
Reeking dung-mouth.
You love-bird.

Reject nothing, sings Walt Whitman.
So you, you go out at last and eat the unmentionable,
In your appetite for affection.

And then you run in to vomit it in my house!
I get my love back.
And I have to clean up after you, filth which even blind Nature
    rejects
From the pit of your stomach;
But you, you snout-face, you reject nothing, you merge so
    much in love
You must eat even that.

Then when I dust you a bit with a juniper twig
You run straight away to live with somebody else,
Fawn before them, and love them as if they were the ones you
    had *really* loved all along.
And they're taken in.
They feel quite tender over you, till you play the same trick on
    them, dirty bitch.

Fidelity! Loyalty! Attachment!
Oh, these are abstractions to your nasty little belly.
You must always be a-waggle with L O V E.
Such a waggle of love you can hardly distinguish one human
    from another.
You love one after another, on one condition, that each one
    loves *you* most.
Democratic little bull-bitch, dirt-eating little swine.

But now, my lass, you've got your Nemesis on your track,
Now you've come sex-alive, and the great ranch dogs are all
    after you.
They're after what they can get, and don't you turn tail!
You loved 'em all so much before, didn't you, loved 'em
    indiscriminate?
You don't love 'em now.
They want something of you, so you squeak and come pelting
    indoors.

Come pelting to me, now the other folk have found you out,
    and the dogs are after you.
Oh yes, you're found out. I heard them kick you out of the
    ranch house:
Get out, you little, soft fool!!

And didn't you turn your eyes up at me then?
And didn't you cringe on the floor like any inkspot!
And crawl away like a black snail!
And doesn't everybody loathe you then!
And aren't your feelings violated, you high-bred little
    love-bitch!

For you're sensitive,
In many ways very finely bred.
But bred in conceit that the world is all for love
Of you, my bitch: till you get so far you eat filth.
Fool, in spite of your pretty ways, and quaint, know-all,
    wrinkled old aunty's face.

So now, what with great Airedale dogs,
And a kick or two,
And a few vomiting bouts,
And a juniper switch,
You look at me for discrimination, don't you?
Look up at me with misgiving in your bulging eyes,
And fear in the smoky whites of your eyes, you nigger;
And you're puzzled,
You think you'd better mind your P's and Q's for a bit,
Your sensitive love-pride being all hurt.

All right, my little bitch.
You learn loyalty rather than loving,
And I'll protect you.

LOBO

MOUNTAIN LION

CLIMBING through the January snow, into the Lobo canyon
Dark grow the spruce trees, blue is the balsam, water sounds
    still unfrozen, and the trail is still evident.

Men!
Two men!
Men! The only animal in the world to fear!

They hesitate.
We hesitate.
They have a gun.
We have no gun.

Then we all advance, to meet.

Two Mexicans, strangers, emerging out of the dark and snow
    and inwardness of the Lobo valley.
What are they doing here on this vanishing trail?

What is he carrying?
Something yellow.
A deer?

Qué tiene, amigo? —
León —

He smiles, foolishly, as if he were caught doing wrong.
And we smile, foolishly, as if we didn't know.
He is quite gentle and dark-faced.

It is a mountain lion,
A long, slim cat, yellow like a lioness.
Dead.

He trapped her this morning, he says, smiling foolishly.

Lift up her face,
Her round, bright face, bright as frost.
Her round, fine-fashioned head, with two dead ears:
And stripes in the brilliant frost of her face, sharp, fine dark
    rays,
Dark, keen, fine rays in the brilliant frost of her face.
Beautiful dead eyes.

Hermoso es!

They go out towards the open;
We go on into the gloom of Lobo.

And above the trees I found her lair,
A hole in the blood-orange brilliant rocks that stick up, a little
    cave.
And bones, and twigs, and a perilous ascent.

So, she will never leap up that way again, with the yellow flash
    of a mountain lion's long shoot!

And her bright striped frost-face will never watch any more,
    out of the shadow of the cave in the blood-orange rock,
Above the trees of the Lobo dark valley-mouth!

Instead, I look out.
And out to the dim of the desert, like a dream, never real;
To the snow of the Sangre de Cristo mountains, the ice of the
    mountains of Picoris,
And near across at the opposite steep of snow, green trees
    motionless standing in snow, like a Christmas toy.

And I think in this empty world there was room for me and a
    mountain lion.
And I think in the world beyond, how easily we might spare a
    million or two of humans
And never miss them.
Yet what a gap in the world, the missing white frost-face of
    that slim yellow mountain lion!

LOBO

❦

1926

❦

RAINBOW

ONE thing that is bow-legged
and can't put its feet together
is the rainbow.

Even if the Lord God shouted
— Attention! —
it couldn't put its feet together.

Yet it's got two feet
as you know,
and two pots of gold
we are told.

What I see
when I look at the rainbow
is one foot in the lap of a woman
and one in the loins of a man.

The feet of the arch
that the Lord God rested the worlds on.

And wide, wide apart,
with nothing but desire between them.

The two feet of the rainbow
want to put themselves together.
But they can't, or there'd be the vicious circle.

So they leap up like a fountain.
He leaps up, she leaps up,
like rockets!
and they curve over.

From the heart a red ray,
from the brow a gold,
from the hips a violet
leaps.

Dark blue the whole desire leaps
brindled with rays
all of the colours
that leap

and lean over
in the arch
of the rainbow.

They will always do it.
The Lord God said so.

If there are pots of gold
they are pails
of the honey of experience
hanging from the shoulders of the rainbow.

But the one thing that is bow-legged
and can't put its feet together
is the rainbow.

Because one foot is the heart of a man
and the other is the heart of a woman.
And these two, as you know,
never meet.

Save they leap
high –
Oh hearts, leap high!
– they touch in mid-heaven like an acrobat
and make a rainbow.

❧

1928–9

❧

from *Pansies*

THE GAZELLE CALF

THE gazelle calf, O my children,
goes behind its mother across the desert,
goes behind its mother on blithe bare foot
requiring no shoes, O my children!

LITTLE FISH

THE tiny fish enjoy themselves
in the sea.
Quick little splinters of life,
their little lives are fun to them
in the sea.

THE MOSQUITO KNOWS

THE mosquito knows full well, small as he is
he's a beast of prey.
But after all
he only takes his bellyful,
he doesn't put my blood in the bank.

SELF-PITY

I NEVER saw a wild thing
sorry for itself.
A small bird will drop frozen dead from a bough
without ever having felt sorry for itself.

SEA-WEED

SEA-WEED sways and sways and swirls
as if swaying were its form of stillness;
and if it flushes against fierce rock
it slips over it as shadows do, without hurting itself.

NEW MOON

THE new moon, of no importance
lingers behind as the yellow sun glares and is gone beyond the
    sea's edge;
earth smokes blue;
the new moon, in cool height above the blushes,
brings a fresh fragrance of heaven to our senses.

FIDELITY

FIDELITY and love are two different things, like a flower and
    a gem.
And love, like a flower, will fade, will change into something
    else
or it would not be flowery.

O flowers they fade because they are moving swiftly; a little
    torrent of life
leaps up to the summit of the stem, gleams, turns over round
    the bend
of the parabola of curved flight,
sinks, and is gone, like a comet curving into the invisible.

O flowers, they are all the time travelling
like comets, and they come into our ken
for a day, for two days, and withdraw, slowly vanish again.

And we, we must take them on the wing, and let them go.
Embalmed flowers are not flowers, immortelles are not
    flowers;
flowers are just a motion, a swift motion, a coloured gesture;
that is their loveliness. And that is love.

But a gem is different. It lasts so much longer than we do
so much much much much longer
that it seems to last for ever.
Yet we know it is flowing away
as flowers are, and we are, only slower.
The wonderful slow flowing of the sapphire!

All flows, and every flow is related to every other flow.
Flowers and sapphires and us, diversely streaming.

In the old days, when sapphires were breathed upon and
    brought forth
during the wild orgasms of chaos
time was much slower, when the rocks came forth.
It took aeons to make a sapphire, aeons for it to pass away.

And a flower it takes a summer.

And man and woman are like the earth, that brings forth
    flowers
in summer, and love, but underneath is rock.
Older than flowers, older than ferns, older than foraminiferæ,
older than plasm altogether is the soul of a man underneath.

And when, throughout all the wild orgasms of love
slowly a gem forms, in the ancient, once-more-molten rocks
of two human hearts, two ancient rocks, a man's heart and a
    woman's,
that is the crystal of peace, the slow hard jewel of trust,
the sapphire of fidelity.
The gem of mutual peace emerging from the wild chaos of
    love.

WHAT AILS THEE?

WHAT ails thee then, woman, what ails thee?
doesn't ter know?

If tha canna say't, come then an' scraight it out on my bosom!
Eh? — Men doesna ha'e bosoms? 'appen not, on'y tha knows
     what I mean.
Come then, tha can scraight it out on my shirt-front an' tha'lt
     feel better.

     — In the first place, I don't scraight.
     And if I did, I certainly couldn't *scraight it out*.
     And if I could, the last place I should choose
     would be your shirt-front
     or your manly bosom either.
     So leave off trying putting the Robbie Burns touch over me
     and kindly hand me the cigarettes
     if you haven't smoked them all,
     which you're much more likely to do
     than to shelter anybody from the cau-auld blast.

THINK —!

IMAGINE what it must have been to have existence
in the wild days when life was sliding whirlwinds, blue-hot
     weights,
in the days called chaos, which left us rocks, and gems!
Think that the sapphire is only alumina, like kitchen pans
crushed utterly, and breathed through and through
with fiery weight and wild life, and coming out
clear and flowery blue!

LIZARD

A LIZARD ran out on a rock and looked up, listening
no doubt to the sounding of the spheres.
And what a dandy fellow! the right toss of a chin for you
and swirl of a tail!

If men were as much men as lizards are lizards
they'd be worth looking at.

SELF-PROTECTION

WHEN science starts to be interpretive
it is more unscientific even than mysticism.

To make self-preservation and self-protection the first law of
      existence
is about as scientific as making suicide the first law of
      existence,
and amounts to very much the same thing.

A nightingale singing at the top of his voice
in neither hiding himself nor preserving himself nor
      propagating his species;
he is giving himself away in every sense of the word;
and obviously, it is the culminating point of his existence.

A tiger is striped and golden for his own glory.
He would certainly be much more invisible if he were
      grey-green.

And I don't suppose the ichthyosaurus sparkled like the
      humming-bird,
no doubt he was khaki-coloured with muddy protective
      coloration,
so why didn't he survive?

As a matter of fact, the only creatures that seem to survive
are those that give themselves away in flash and sparkle
and gay flicker of joyful life;
those that go glittering abroad
with a bit of splendour.

Even mice play quite beautifully at shadows,
and some of them are brilliantly piebald.

I expect the dodo looked like a clod,
a drab and dingy bird.

WAGES

THE wages of work is cash.
The wages of cash is want more cash.
The wages of want more cash is vicious competition.
The wages of vicious competition is – the world we live in.

The work-cash-want circle is the viciousest circle
that ever turned men into fiends.

Earning a wage is a prison occupation
and a wage-earner is a sort of gaol-bird.

Earning a salary is a prison overseer's job
a gaoler instead of a gaol-bird.

Living on our income is strolling grandly outside the prison
in terror lest you have to go in. And since the work-prison
        covers
almost every scrap of the living earth, you stroll up and down
on a narrow beat, about the same as a prisoner taking exercise.

This is called universal freedom.

A SANE REVOLUTION

If you make a revolution, make it for fun,
don't make it in ghastly seriousness,
don't do it in deadly earnest,
do it for fun.

Don't do it because you hate people,
do it just to spit in their eye.

Don't do it for the money,
do it and be damned to the money.

Don't do it for equality,
do it because we've got too much equality
and it would be fun to upset the apple-cart
and see which way the apples would go a-rolling.

Don't do it for the working classes.
Do it so that we can all of us be little aristocracies on our own
and kick our heels like jolly escaped asses.

Don't do it, anyhow, for international Labour.
Labour is the one thing a man has had too much of.
Let's abolish labour, let's have done with labouring!
Work can be fun, and men can enjoy it; then it's not labour.
Let's have it so! Let's make a revolution for fun!

NEMESIS

The nemesis that awaits our civilisation
is social insanity
which in the end is always homicidal.

Sanity means the wholeness of the consciousness.
And our society is only part conscious, like an idiot.

If we do not rapidly open all the doors of consciousness
and freshen the putrid little space in which we are cribbed
the sky-blue walls of our unventilated heaven
will be bright red with blood.

NOVEMBER BY THE SEA

Now in November nearer comes the sun
down the abandoned heaven.

As the dark closes round him, he draws nearer
as if for our company.

At the base of the lower brain
the sun in me declines to his winter solstice
and darts a few gold rays
back to the old year's sun across the sea.

A few gold rays thickening down to red
as the sun of my soul is setting
setting fierce and undaunted, wintry
but setting, setting behind the sounding sea between my ribs.

The wide sea wins, and the dark
winter, and the great day-sun, and the sun in my soul
sinks, sinks to setting and the winter solstice
downward, they race in decline
my sun, and the great gold sun.

FIRE

Fire is dearer to us than love or food,
hot, hurrying, yet it burns if you touch it.

What we ought to do
is not to add our love together, or our goodwill, or any of that,

for we're sure to bring in a lot of lies,
but our fire, our elemental fire
so that it rushes up in a huge blaze like a phallus into hollow
    space
and fecundates the zenith and the nadir
and sends off millions of sparks of new atoms
and singes us, and burns the house down.

BEAUTIFUL OLD AGE

IT ought to be lovely to be old
to be full of the peace that comes of experience
and wrinkled ripe fulfilment.

The wrinkled smile of completeness that follows a life
lived undaunted and unsoured with accepted lies.
If people lived without accepting lies
they would ripen like apples, and be scented like pippins
in their old age.

Soothing, old people should be, like apples
when one is tired of love.
Fragrant like yellowing leaves, and dim with the soft
stillness and satisfaction of autumn.

And a girl should say:
It must be wonderful to live and grow old.
Look at my mother, how rich and still she is!

And a young man should think: By Jove
my father has faced all weathers, but it's been a life!

DESIRE IS DEAD

DESIRE may be dead
and still a man can be
a meeting place for sun and rain
wonder outwaiting pain
as in a wintry tree.

GLORY

GLORY is of the sun, too, and the sun of suns,
and down the shafts of his splendid pinions
run tiny rivers of peace.

Most of his time, the tiger pads and slouches in a burning
    peace.
And the small hawk high up turns round on the slow pivot of
    peace.
Peace comes from behind the sun, with the peregrine falcon,
    and the owl.
Yet all of these drink blood.

WHAT WOULD YOU FIGHT FOR?

I AM not sure I would always fight for my life.
Life might not be worth fighting for.

I am not sure I would always fight for my wife.
A wife isn't always worth fighting for.

Nor my children, nor my country, nor my fellow-men.
It all depends whether I found them worth fighting for.

The only thing men invariably fight for
is their money. But I doubt if I'd fight for mine, anyhow not to
    shed a lot of blood over it.

Yet one thing I do fight for, tooth and nail, all the time.
And that is my bit of inward peace, where I am at one with
    myself.

And I must say, I am often worsted.

GOOD HUSBANDS MAKE UNHAPPY WIVES

GOOD husbands make unhappy wives
so do bad husbands, just as often;
but the unhappiness of a wife with a good husband
is much more devastating
than the unhappiness of a wife with a bad husband.

TO WOMEN, AS FAR AS I'M CONCERNED

THE feelings I don't have, I don't have.
The feelings I don't have, I won't say I have.
The feelings you say you have, you don't have.
The feelings you would like us both to have, we neither of us
    have.

The feelings people ought to have, they never have.
If people say they've got feelings, you may be pretty sure they
    haven't got them.

So if you want either of us to feel anything at all
you'd better abandon all idea of feelings altogether.

WHEN I WENT TO THE CIRCUS

WHEN I went to the circus that had pitched on the waste lot
it was full of uneasy people
frightened of the bare earth and the temporary canvas
and the smell of horses and other beasts
instead of merely the smell of man.

Monkeys rode rather grey and wizened
on curly plump piebald ponies
and the children uttered a little cry —
and dogs jumped through hoops and turned somersaults
and then the geese scuttled in in a little flock
and round the ring they went to the sound of the whip
then doubled, and back, with a funny up-flutter of wings —
and the children suddenly shouted out.

Then came the hush again, like a hush of fear.

The tight-rope lady, pink and blonde and nude-looking, with a
     few gold spangles
footed cautiously out on the rope, turned prettily, spun round
bowed, and lifted her foot in her hand, smiled, swung her
     parasol
to another balance, tripped round, poised, and slowly sank
her handsome thighs down, down, till she slept her splendid
     body on the rope.
When she rose, tilting her parasol, and smiled at the cautious
     people
they cheered, but nervously.

The trapeze man, slim and beautiful and like a fish in the air
swung great curves through the upper space, and came down
     like a star.
— And the people applauded, with hollow, frightened
     applause.

The elephants, huge and grey, loomed their curved bulk
     through the dusk
and sat up, taking strange postures, showing the pink soles of
     their feet
and curling their precious live trunks like ammonites
and moving always with soft slow precision
as when a great ship moves to anchor.
The people watched and wondered, and seemed to resent the
     mystery that lies in beasts.

Horses, gay horses, swirling round and plaiting
in a long line, their heads laid over each other's necks;
they were happy, they enjoyed it;
all the creatures seemed to enjoy the game
in the circus, with their circus people.

But the audience, compelled to wonder
compelled to admire the bright rhythms of moving bodies
compelled to see the delicate skill of flickering human bodies
flesh flamey and a little heroic, even in a tumbling clown,
they were not really happy.
There was no gushing response, as there is at the film.

When modern people see the carnal body dauntless and
        flickering gay
playing among the elements neatly, beyond competition
and displaying no personality,
modern people are depressed.

Modern people feel themselves at a disadvantage.
They know they have no bodies that could play among the
        elements.
They have only their personalities, that are best seen flat, on
        the film,
flat personalities in two dimensions, imponderable and
        touchless.

And they grudge the circus people the swooping gay weight of
        limbs
that flower in mere movement,
and they grudge them the immediate, physical understanding
        they have with their circus beasts,
and they grudge them their circus life altogether.

Yet the strange, almost frightened shout of delight that comes
        now and then from the children
shows that the children vaguely know how cheated they are of
        their birthright
in the bright wild circus flesh.

TWO PERFORMING ELEPHANTS

He stands with his forefeet on the drum
and the other, the old one, the pallid hoary female
must creep her great bulk beneath the bridge of him.

On her knees, in utmost caution
all agog, and curling up her trunk
she edges through without upsetting him.
Triumph! the ancient pig-tailed monster!

When her trick is to climb over him
with what shadow-like slow carefulness
she skims him, sensitive
as shadows from the ages gone and perished
in touching him, and planting her round feet.

While the wispy, modern children, half-afraid
watch silent. The looming of the hoary, far-gone ages
is too much for them.

TO LET GO OR TO HOLD ON –?

Shall we let go,
and allow the soul to find its level
downwards, ebbing downwards, ebbing downwards to the
    flood?
till the head floats tilted like a bottle forward tilted
on the sea, with no message in it; and the body is submerged
heavy and swaying like a whale recovering
from wounds, below the deep black wave?
like a whale recovering its velocity and strength
under the cold black wave.

Or else, or else
shall a man brace himself up
and lift his face and set his breast
and go forth to change the world?

gather his will and his energy together
and fling himself in effort after effort
upon the world, to bring a change to pass?

Tell me first, O tell me,
will the dark flood of our day's annihilation
swim deeper, deeper, till it leaves no peak emerging?
Shall we be lost, all of us
and gone like weed, like weed, like eggs of fishes,
like sperm of whales, like germs of the great dead past
into which the creative future shall blow strange, unknown
      forms?
Are we nothing, already, but the lapsing of a great dead past?
Is the best that we are but sperm, loose sperm, like the sperm
      of fishes
that drifts upon time and chaos, till some unknown future
      takes it up
and is fecund with a new Day of new creatures? different from
      us.

Or is our shattered Argosy, our leaking ark
at this moment scraping tardy Ararat?
Have we got to get down and clear away the debris
of a swamped civilisation, and start a new world for man
that will blossom forth the whole of human nature?

Must we hold on, hold on
and go ahead with what is human nature
and make a new job of the human world?

Or can we let it go?
O, can we let it go,
and leave it to some nature that is more than human
to use the sperm of what's worth while in us
and thus eliminate us?
Is the time come for humans
now to begin to disappear,

leaving it to the vast revolutions of creative chaos
to bring forth creatures that are an improvement on humans,
as the horse was an improvement on the ichthyosaurus?

Must we hold on?
Or can we now let go?

Or is it even possible we must do both?

SWAN

FAR-OFF
at the core of space
at the quick of time
beats
and goes still
the great swan upon the waters of all endings
the swan within vast chaos, within the electron.

For us
no longer he swims calmly
nor clacks across the forces furrowing a great gay trail
of happy energy,
nor is he nesting passive upon the atoms,
nor flying north desolative icewards
to the sleep of ice,
nor feeding in the marshes,
nor honking horn-like into the twilight. –

But he stoops, now
in the dark
upon us;
he is treading our women
and we men are put out
as the vast white bird
furrows our featherless women
with unknown shocks
and stamps his black marsh-feet on their white and marshy flesh.

LEDA

COME not with kisses
not with caresses
of hands and lips and murmurings;
come with a hiss of wings
and sea-touch tip of a beak
and treading of wet, webbed, wave-working feet
into the marsh-soft belly.

GIVE US GODS

GIVE us gods, Oh give them us!
Give us gods.
We are so tired of men
and motor-power. —

But not gods grey-bearded and dictatorial,
nor yet that pale young man afraid of fatherhood
shelving substance on to the woman, Madonna mia! shabby
    virgin!
nor gusty Jove, with his eye on immortal tarts,
nor even the musical, suave young fellow
wooing boys and beauty.

Give us gods
give us something else —

Beyond the great bull that bellowed through space, and got his
    throat cut.
Beyond even that eagle, that phœnix, hanging over the gold
    egg of all things,
further still, before the curled horns of the ram stepped forth
or the stout swart beetle rolled the globe of dung in which man
    should hatch,
or even the sly gold serpent fatherly lifted his head off the earth
    to think —

Give us gods before these —
Thou shalt have other gods before these.

Where the waters end in marshes
swims the wild swan
sweeps the high goose above the mists
honking in the gloom the honk of procreation from such
     throats.

Mists
where the electron behaves and misbehaves as it will,
where the forces tie themselves up into knots of atoms
and come untied;
mists
of mistiness complicated into knots and clots that barge about
and bump on one another and explode into more mist, or
     don't,
mist of energy most scientific —
But give us gods!

Look then
where the father of all things swims in a mist of atoms
electrons and energies, quantums and relativities
mists, wreathing mists,
like a wild swan, or a goose, whose honk goes through my
     bladder.
And in the dark unscientific I feel the drum-winds of his wings
and the drip of his cold, webbed feet, mud-black
brush over my face as he goes
to seek the women in the dark, our women, our weird women
     whom he treads
with dreams and thrusts that make them cry in their sleep.

Gods, do you ask for gods?
Where there is woman there is swan.

Do you think, scientific man, you'll be father of your own
    babies?
Don't imagine it.
There'll be babies born that are cygnets, O my soul!
young wild swans!
And babies of women will come out young wild geese, O my
    heart!
the geese that saved Rome, and will lose London.

WON'T IT BE STRANGE –?

WON'T it be strange, when the nurse brings the new-born
    infant
to the proud father, and shows its little, webbed greenish feet
made to smite the waters behind it?
or the round, wild vivid eye of a wild-goose staring
out of fathomless skies and seas?
or when it utters that undaunted little bird-cry
of one who will settle on ice-bergs, and honk across the
    Nile? –

And when the father says: This is none of mine!
Woman, where got you this little beast? –
will there be a whistle of wings in the air, and an icy draught?
will the singing of swans, high up, high up, invisible
break the drums of his ears
and leave him forever listening for the answer?

RELATIVITY

I LIKE relativity and quantum theories
because I don't understand them
and they make me feel as if space shifted about like a swan that
    can't settle,
refusing to sit still and be measured;

and as if the atom were an impulsive thing
always changing its mind.

NOTTINGHAM'S NEW UNIVERSITY

In Nottingham, that dismal town
where I went to school and college,
they've built a new university
for a new dispensation of knowledge.

Built it most grand and cakeily
out of the noble loot
derived from shrewd cash-chemistry
by good Sir Jesse Boot.

Little I thought, when I was a lad
and turned my modest penny
over on Boot's Cash-Chemist's counter,
that Jesse, by turning many

millions of similar honest pence
over, would make a pile
that would rise at last and blossom out
in grand and cakey style

into a university
where smart men would dispense
doses of smart cash-chemistry
in language of common-sense!

That future Nottingham lads would be
cash-chemically B. Sc.
that Nottingham lights would rise and say:
– By Boots I am M. A.

From this I learn, though I knew it before
that culture has her roots
in the deep dung of cash, and lore
is a last offshoot of Boots.

WHATEVER MAN MAKES

WHATEVER man makes and makes it live
lives because of the life put into it.
A yard of India muslin is alive with Hindu life.
And a Navajo woman, weaving her rug in the pattern of her
    dream
must run the pattern out in a little break at the end
so that her soul can come out, back to her.

But in the odd pattern, like snake-marks on the sand
it leaves its trail.

WE ARE TRANSMITTERS

A s we live, we are transmitters of life.
And when we fail to transmit life, life fails to flow through us.

That is part of the mystery of sex, it is a flow onwards.
Sexless people transmit nothing.

And if, as we work, we can transmit life into our work,
life, still more life, rushes into us to compensate, to be ready
and we ripple with life through the days.

Even if it is a woman making an apple dumpling, or a man a
    stool,
if life goes into the pudding, good is the pudding
good is the stool,
content is the woman, with fresh life rippling in to her,
content is the man.

Give, and it shall be given unto you
is still the truth about life.
But giving life is not so easy.
It doesn't mean handing it out to some mean fool, or letting
     the living dead eat you up.
It means kindling the life-quality where it was not,
even if it's only in the whiteness of a washed pocket-
     handkerchief.

RED-HERRING

My father was a working man
     and a collier was he,
at six in the morning they turned him down
     and they turned him up for tea.

My mother was a superior soul
     a superior soul was she,
cut out to play a superior role
     in the god-damn bourgeoisie.

We children were the in-betweens
     little non-descripts were we,
indoors we called each other *you*,
     outside, it was *tha* and *thee*.

But time has fled, our parents are dead,
     we've risen in the world all three;
but still we are in-betweens, we tread
     between the devil and the deep sad sea.

I am a member of the bourgeoisie
     and a servant-maid brings me my tea —
But I'm always longing for someone to say:
     'ark 'ere, lad! atween thee an' me

they're a' a b——— d— lot o' ———s,
    an' I reckon it's nowt but right
we should start an' kick their —— ses for 'em
    an' tell 'em to ————.

NO! MR LAWRENCE!

No, Mr Lawrence, it's not like that!
I don't mind telling you
I know a thing or two about love,
perhaps more than you do.

And what I know is that you make it
too nice, too beautiful.
It's not like that, you know; you fake it.
It's really rather dull.

THE LITTLE WOWSER

THERE is a little wowser
    John Thomas by name,
and for every bloomin', mortal thing
    that little blighter's to blame.

It was 'im as made the first mistake
    of putting us in the world,
forcin' us out of the unawake,
    an' makin' us come uncurled.

And then when you're gettin' nicely on
    an' life seems to begin,
that little bleeder comes bustin' in
    with: Hello boy! what about sin?

An' then he leads you by the nose
 after a lot o' women
as strips you stark as a monkey nut
 an' leaves you never a trimmin'.

An' then somebody has ter marry you
 to put him through 'is paces;
then when John Thomas don't worry you,
 it's your wife, wi' her airs an' graces.

I think of all the little brutes
 as ever was invented
that little cod's the holy worst.
 I've chucked him, I've repented.

CONUNDRUMS

TELL me a word
that you've often heard,
yet it makes you squint
if you see it in print!

Tell me a thing
that you've often seen,
yet if put in a book
it makes you turn green!

Tell me a thing
that you often do,
which, described in a story
shocks you through and through!

Tell me what's wrong
with words or with you
that you don't mind the thing
yet the name is taboo.

WILLY WET-LEG

I CAN'T stand Willy wet-leg,
can't stand him at any price.
He's resigned, and when you hit him
he lets you hit him twice.

CANVASSING FOR THE ELECTION

— EXCUSE me, but are you a superior person?
— I beg your pardon?
— Oh, I'm sure you'll understand. We're making a census of all
the *really* patriotic people — the right sort of people, you know
— of course you understand what I mean — so *would* you mind
giving me your word? — and signing here, please — that you *are*
a superior person — that's all we need to know —
— Really, I don't know what you take me for!
— Yes, I know! It's too bad! Of course it's perfectly superfluous
to ask, but the League insists. Thank you so much! No, sign
here, please, and there I countersign. That's right! Yes, that's
all! — *I declare I am a superior person* —. Yes, exactly! and here
I countersign your declaration. It's so simple, and really, it's
all we need to know about anybody. And do you know, I've
never been denied a signature! We English *are* a solid people,
after all. This proves it. Quite! Thank you so much! We're
getting on simply splendidly — and it *is* a comfort, isn't it? —

ANDRAITX – POMEGRANATE FLOWERS

IT is June, it is June
the pomegranates are in flower,
the peasants are bending cutting the bearded wheat.

The pomegranates are in flower
beside the high road, past the deathly dust,
and even the sea is silent in the sun.

Short gasps of flame in the green of night, way off
the pomegranates are in flower,
small sharp red fires in the night of leaves.

And noon is suddenly dark, is lustrous, is silent and dark
men are unseen, beneath the shading hats;
only, from out the foliage of the secret loins
red flamelets here and there reveal
a man, a woman there.

THE HEART OF MAN

THERE is the other universe, of the heart of man
that we know nothing of, that we dare not explore.

A strange grey distance separates
our pale mind still from the pulsing continent
of the heart of man.

Fore-runners have barely landed on the shore
and no man knows, no woman knows
the mystery of the interior
when darker still than Congo or Amazon
flow the heart's rivers of fulness, desire and distress.

MORAL CLOTHING

WHEN I am clothed I am a moral man,
and unclothed, the word has no meaning for me.

When I put on my coat, my coat has pockets
and in the pockets are things I require,
so I wish no man to pick my pocket
and I will pick the pocket of no man.

A man's business is one of his pockets, his bank account too
his credit, his name, his wife even may be just another of his
    pockets.
And I loathe the thought of being a pilferer
a pick-pocket.
That is why business seems to me despicable,
and most love-affairs, just sneak-thief pocket-picking
of dressed-up people.

When I stand in my shirt I have no pockets
therefore no morality of pockets;
but still my nakedness is clothed with responsibility
towards those near and dear to me, my very next of kin.
I am not yet alone.

Only when I am stripped stark naked I am alone
and without morals, and without immorality.
The invisible gods have no moral truck with us.

And if stark naked I approach a fellow-man or fellow-woman
they must be naked too,
and none of us must expect morality of each other:
I am that I am, take it or leave it.
Offer me nothing but that which you are, stark and strange.
Let there be no accommodation at this issue.

THE CHURCH

IF I was a member of the Church of Rome
I should advocate reform:
the marriage of priests
the priests to wear rose-colour or magenta in the streets
to teach the Resurrection in the flesh
to start the year on Easter Sunday
to add the mystery of Joy-in-Resurrection to the Mass
to inculcate the new conception of the Risen Man.

FATALITY

No one, not even God, can put back a leaf on to a tree
once it has fallen off.

And no one, not God nor Christ nor any other
can put back a human life into connection with the living
        cosmos
once the connection has been broken
and the person has become finally self-centred.

Death alone, through the long processes of disintegration
can melt the detached life back
through the dark Hades at the roots of the tree
into the circulating sap, once more, of the tree of life.

HEALING

I AM not a mechanism, an assembly of various sections.
And it is not because the mechanism is working wrongly, that I
        am ill.
I am ill because of wounds to the soul, to the deep emotional
        self
and the wounds to the soul take a long, long time, only time
        can help

and patience, and a certain difficult repentance
long, difficult repentance, realisation of life's mistake, and the
    freeing oneself
from the endless repetition of the mistake
which mankind at large has chosen to sanctify.

MODERN PRAYER

ALMIGHTY Mammon, make me rich!
Make me rich quickly, with never a hitch
in my fine prosperity! Kick those in the ditch
who hinder me, Mammon, great son of a bitch!

BELLS

THE Mohammedans say that the sound of bells
especially big ones, is obscene,

That hard clapper striking in a hard mouth
and resounding after with a long hiss of insistence
is obscene.

Yet bells call the Christians to God
especially clapper bells, hard tongues wagging in hard mouths,
metal hitting on metal, to enforce our attention . . .
and bring us to God.

The soft thudding of drums
of fingers or fists or soft-skinned sticks upon the stretched
    membrane of sound
sends summons in the old hollows of the sun.

And the accumulated splashing of a gong
where tissue plunges into bronze with wide wild circles of
    sound and leaves off,
belongs to the bamboo thickets, and the drake in the air flying
    past.

And the sound of a blast through the sea-curved core of a shell
when a black priest blows on a conch,
and the dawn-cry from a minaret, God is Great,
and the calling of the old Red Indian high on the pueblo roof
whose voice flies on and on, calling like a swan
singing between the sun and the marsh,
on and on, like a dark-faced bird singing alone
singing to the men below, the fellow-tribesmen
who go by without pausing, soft-foot, without listening, yet
    who hear:
there are other ways of summons, crying: Listen! Listen! Come
    near!

THE TRIUMPH OF THE MACHINE

THEY talk of the triumph of the machine,
but the machine will never triumph.

Out of the thousands and thousands of centuries of man
the unrolling of ferns, white tongues of the acanthus lapping at
    the sun,
for one sad century
machines have triumphed, rolled us hither and thither,
shaking the lark's nest till the eggs have broken.
Shaken the marshes till the geese have gone
and the wild swans flown away singing the swan-song of us.

Hard, hard on the earth the machines are rolling,
but through some hearts they will never roll.

The lark nests in his heart
and the white swan swims in the marshes of his loins,
and through the wide prairies of his breast a young bull herds
    his cows,
lambs frisk among the daisies of his brain.

And at last
all these creatures that cannot die, driven back
into the uttermost corners of the soul,
will send up the wild cry of despair.

The trilling lark in a wild despair will trill down arrows from
    the sky,
the swan will beat the waters in rage, white rage of an enraged
    swan,
even the lambs will stretch forth their necks like serpents,
like snakes of hate, against the man in the machine:
even the shaking white poplar will dazzle like splinters of glass
    against him.

And against this inward revolt of the native creatures of the
    soul
mechanical man, in triumph seated upon the seat of his
    machine
will be powerless, for no engine can reach into the marshes
    and depths of a man.

So mechanical man in triumph seated upon the seat of his
    machine
will be driven mad from within himself, and sightless, and on
    that day
the machines will turn to run into one another
traffic will tangle up in a long-drawn-out crash of collision
and engines will rush at the solid houses, the edifice of our life
will rock in the shock of the mad machine, and the house will
    come down.

Then, far beyond the ruin, in the far, in the ultimate, remote
    places
the swan will lift up again his flattened, smitten head
and look round, and rise, and on the great vaults of his wings
will sweep round and up to greet the sun with a silky glitter of
    a new day
and the lark will follow trilling, angerless again,

and the lambs will bite off the heads of the daisies for very
     friskiness.
But over the middle of the earth will be the smoky ruin of iron
the triumph of the machine.

LEAVES OF GRASS, FLOWERS OF GRASS

LEAVES of grass, what about leaves of grass?
Grass blossoms, grass has flowers, flowers of grass
dusty pollen of grass, tall grass in its midsummer maleness,
hay-seed and tiny grain of grass, graminiferae
not far from the lily, the considerable lily;

even the blue-grass blossoms;
even the bison knew it;
even the stupidest farmer gathers his hay in bloom, in blossom
just before it seeds.

Only the best matters; even the cow knows it;
grass in blossom, blossoming grass, risen to its height and its
     natural pride
in its own splendour and its own feathery maleness
the grass, the grass.

Leaves of grass, what are leaves of grass, when at its best grass
     blossoms.

WE DIE TOGETHER

OH, when I think of the industrial millions, when I see some of
     them,
a weight comes over me heavier than leaden linings of coffins
and I almost cease to exist, weighed down to extinction
and sunk into a depression that almost blots me out.

Then I say to myself: Am I also dead? is that the truth?
Then I know
that with so many dead men in mills
I too am almost dead.
I know the unliving factory-hand, living-dead millions
is unliving me, living-dead me,
I, with them, am living-dead, mechanical at the machine.

And enshrouded in the vast corpse of the industrial millions
embedded in them, I look out on the sunshine of the South.

And though the pomegranate has red flowers outside the
        window
and oleander is hot with perfume under the afternoon sun
and I am 'il Signore' and they love me here,
yet I am a mill-hand in Leeds
and the death of the Black Country is upon me
and I am wrapped in the lead of a coffin-lining, the living death
        of my fellow men.

THE GODS! THE GODS!

PEOPLE were bathing and posturing themselves on the beach
and all was dreary, great robot limbs, robot breasts
robot voices, robot even the gay umbrellas.

But a woman, shy and alone, was washing herself under a tap
and the glimmer of the presence of the gods was like lilies,
and like water-lilies.

NAME THE GODS!

I REFUSE to name the gods, because they have no name.
I refuse to describe the gods, because they have no form nor
        shape nor substance.

Ah, but the simple ask for images!
Then for a time at least, they must do without.

But all the time I see the gods:
the man who is mowing the tall white corn,
suddenly, as it curves, as it yields, the white wheat
and sinks down with a swift rustle, and a strange, falling
    flatness,
ah! the gods, the swaying body of god!
ah the fallen stillness of god, autumnus, and it is only July
the pale-gold flesh of Priapus dropping asleep.

THERE ARE NO GODS

THERE are no gods, and you can please yourself
have a game of tennis, go out in the car, do some shopping, sit
    and talk, talk, talk
with a cigarette browning your fingers.

There are no gods, and you can please yourself —
go and please yourself —

But leave me alone, leave me alone, to myself!
and then in the room, whose is the presence
that makes the air so still and lovely to me?

Who is it that softly touches the sides of my breast
and touches me over the heart
so that my heart beats soothed, soothed, soothed and at peace?

Who is it smooths the bed-sheets like the cool
smooth ocean where the fishes rest on edge
in their own dream?

Who is it that clasps and kneads my naked feet, till they
    unfold,
till all is well, till all is utterly well? the lotus-lilies of the feet!

I tell you, it is no woman, it is no man, for I am alone.
And I fall asleep with the gods, the gods
that are not, or that are
according to the soul's desire,
like a pool into which we plunge, or do not plunge.

RETORT TO WHITMAN

AND whoever walks a mile full of false sympathy
walks to the funeral of the whole human race.

RETORT TO JESUS

AND whoever forces himself to love anybody
begets a murderer in his own body.

SENSE OF TRUTH

YOU must fuse mind and wit with all the senses
before you can feel truth.
And if you can't feel truth you can't have any other
satisfactory sensual experience.

EDITORIAL OFFICE

APPLICANT for post as literary critic: Here are my credentials,
    Sir! –
Editor: Er – quite. But – er – biologically! Have you been fixed?
    – *arrangé* – you understand what I mean?
Applicant: I'm afraid I don't.
Editor (sternly): Have you been made safe for the great British
    Public? Has everything objectionable been removed from
    you?
Applicant: In what way, quite?

Editor: By surgical operation. Did your parents have you
    sterilised?
Applicant: I don't think so, Sir. I'm afraid not.
Editor: Good morning! Don't trouble to call again. We have the
    welfare of the British Public at heart.

THE ENGLISH ARE SO NICE!

THE English are so nice
so awfully nice
they're the nicest people in the world.
And what's more, they're very nice about being nice
about your being nice as well!
If you're not nice, they soon make you feel it.

Americans and French and Germans and so on
they're all very well
but they're not *really* nice, you know.
They're not nice in *our* sense of the word, are they now?

That's why one doesn't have to take them seriously.
We must be nice to them, of course,
of course, naturally –
But it doesn't really matter what you say to them,
they don't really understand –
you can just say anything to them:
be nice, you know, just be nice –
but you must never take them seriously, they wouldn't
    understand
just be nice, you know! oh, fairly nice,
not too nice of course, they take advantage –
but nice enough, just nice enough
to let them feel they're not quite as nice as they might be.

TERRA INCOGNITA

THERE are vast realms of consciousness still undreamed of
vast ranges of experience, like the humming of unseen harps,
we know nothing of, within us.
Oh when man has escaped from the barbed-wire entanglement
of his own ideas and his own mechanical devices
there is a marvellous rich world of contact and sheer fluid
    beauty
and fearless face-to-face awareness of now-naked life
and me, and you, and other men and women
and grapes, and ghouls, and ghosts and green moonlight
and ruddy-orange limbs stirring the limbo
of the unknown air, and eyes so soft
softer than the space between the stars,
and all things, and nothing, and being and not-being
alternately palpitant;
when at last we escape the barbed-wire enclosure
of *Know Thyself*, knowing we can never know,
we can but touch, and wonder, and ponder, and make our
    effort
and dangle in a last fastidious fine delight
as the fuchsia does, dangling her reckless drop
of purple after so much putting forth
and slow mounting marvel of a little tree.

INNOCENT ENGLAND

    OH what a pity, Oh! don't you agree
    that figs aren't found in the land of the free!

    Fig-trees don't grow in my native land;
    there's never a fig-leaf near at hand

    when you want one; so I did without;
    and that is what the row's about.

Virginal, pure policemen came
and hid their faces for very shame,

while they carried the shameless things away
to gaol, to be hid from the light of day.

And Mr Mead, that old, old lily
said: 'Gross! coarse! hideous!' – and I, like a silly

thought he meant the faces of the police-court officials,
and how right he was, and I signed my initials

to confirm what he said; but alas, he meant
my pictures, and on the proceedings went.

The upshot was, my pictures must burn
that English artists might finally learn

when they painted a nude, to put a *cache sexe* on,
a cache sexe, a cache sexe, or else begone!

A fig leaf; or, if you cannot find it
a wreath of mist, with nothing behind it.

A wreath of mist is the usual thing
in the north, to hide where the turtles sing.

Though they never sing, they never sing,
don't you dare to suggest such a thing

or Mr Mead will be after you.
– But what a pity I never knew

A wreath of English mist would do
as a cache sexe! I'd have put a whole fog.

But once and forever barks the old dog,
so my pictures are in prison, instead of in the Zoo.

FOR A MOMENT

FOR a moment, at evening, tired, as he stepped off the
    tram-car,
— the young tram-conductor in a blue uniform, to himself
    forgotten, —
and lifted his face up, with blue eyes looking at the electric rod
    which he was going to turn round,
for a moment, pure in the yellow evening light, he was
    Hyacinthus.

In the green garden darkened the shadow of coming rain
and a girl ran swiftly, laughing breathless, taking in her
    white washing
in rapid armfuls from the line, tossing it in the basket,
and so rapidly, and so flashing, fleeing before the rain
for a moment she was Io, Io, who fled from Zeus, or the
    Danaë.

When I was waiting and not thinking, sitting at a table on the
    hotel terrace
I saw suddenly coming towards me, lit up and uplifted with
    pleasure
advancing with the slow-swiftness of a ship backing her white
    sails into port
the woman who looks for me in the world
and for the moment she was Isis, gleaming, having found her
    Osiris.

For a moment, as he looked at me through his spectacles
pondering, yet eager, the broad and thick-set Italian who
    works in with me,
for a moment he was the Centaur, the wise yet horse-hoofed
    Centaur
in whom I can trust.

THOUGHT

Thought, I love thought.
But not the juggling and twisting of already existent ideas
I despise that self-important game.
Thought is the welling up of unknown life into consciousness,
Thought is the testing of statements on the touchstone of the
    conscience,
Thought is gazing on to the face of life, and reading what can
    be read,
Thought is pondering over experience, and coming to a
    conclusion.
Thought is not a trick, or an exercise, or a set of dodges,
Thought is a man in his wholeness wholly attending.

GLADNESS OF DEATH

Oh death
about you I know nothing, nothing –
about the afterwards
as a matter of fact, we know nothing.

Yet oh death, oh death
also I know so much about you
the knowledge is within me, without being a matter of fact.

And so I know
after the painful, painful experience of dying
there comes an after-gladness, a strange joy
in a great adventure
oh the great adventure of death, where Thomas Cook cannot
    guide us.

I have always wanted to be as the flowers are
so unhampered in their living and dying,
and in death I believe I shall be as the flowers are.

I shall blossom like a dark pansy, and be delighted
there among the dark sun-rays of death.
I can feel myself unfolding in the dark sunshine of death
to something flowery and fulfilled, and with a strange sweet
    perfume.

Men prevent one another from being men
but in the great spaces of death
the winds of the afterwards kiss us into blossom of manhood.

GOD IS BORN

THE history of the cosmos
is the history of the struggle of becoming.
When the dim flux of unformed life
struggled, convulsed back and forth upon itself,
and broke at last into light and dark
came into existence as light,
came into existence as cold shadow
then every atom of the cosmos trembled with delight.
Behold, God is born!
He is bright light!
He is pitch dark and cold!

And in the great struggle of intangible chaos
when, at a certain point, a drop of water began to drip
    downwards
and a breath of vapour began to wreathe up
Lo again the shudder of bliss through all the atoms!
Oh, God is born!
Behold, he is born wet!
Look, He hath movement upward! He spirals!
And so, in the great aeons of accomplishment and débâcle
from time to time the wild crying of every electron:
Lo! God is born!

When sapphires cooled out of molten chaos:
See, God is born! He is blue, he is deep blue, he is forever blue!
When gold lay shining threading the cooled-off rock:
God is born! God is born! bright yellow and ductile He is
    born.

When the little eggy amoeba emerged out of foam and
    nowhere
then all the electrons held their breath:
Ach! Ach! Now indeed God is born! He twinkles within.

When from a world of mosses and of ferns
at last the narcissus lifted a tuft of five-point stars
and dangled them in the atmosphere,
then every molecule of creation jumped and clapped its hands:
God is born! God is born perfumed and dangling and with a
    little cup!

Throughout the aeons, as the lizard swirls his tail finer than
    water,
as the peacock turns to the sun, and could not be more
    splendid,
as the leopard smites the small calf with a spangled paw,
    perfect.
the universe trembles: God is born! God is here!

And when at last man stood on two legs and wondered,
then there was a hush of suspense at the core of every electron:
Behold, now very God is born!
God Himself is born!

And so we see, God is not
until he is born.

And also we see
there is no end to the birth of God.

FLOWERS AND MEN

FLOWERS achieve their own floweriness and it is a miracle.
Men don't achieve their own manhood, alas, oh alas! alas!

All I want of you, men and women,
all I want of you
is that you shall achieve your own beauty
as the flowers do.

Oh leave off saying I want you to be savages.
Tell me, is the gentian savage, at the top of its coarse stem?
Oh what in you can answer to this blueness?

from *Last Poems*

THE ARGONAUTS

THEY are not dead, they are not dead!
Now that the sun, like a lion licks his paws
and goes slowly down the hill:
now that the moon, who remembers, and only cares
that we should be lovely in the flesh, with bright, crescent feet,
pauses near the crest of the hill, climbing slowly, like a queen
looking down on the lion as he retreats –

Now the sea is the Argonauts' sea, and in the dawn
Odysseus calls the commands, as he steers past those foamy
        islands;
wait, wait, don't bring me the coffee yet, nor the *pain grillé*.
The dawn is not off the sea, and Odysseus' ships
have not yet passed the islands, I must watch them still.

MIDDLE OF THE WORLD

THIS sea will never die, neither will it ever grow old
nor cease to be blue, nor in the dawn
cease to lift up its hills
and let the slim black ship of Dionysos come sailing in
with grape-vines up the mast, and dolphins leaping.

What do I care if the smoking ships
of the P. & O. and the Orient Line and all the other stinkers
cross like clock-work the Minoan distance!
They only cross, the distance never changes.

And now that the moon who gives men glistening bodies
is in her exaltation, and can look down on the sun
I see descending from the ships at dawn
slim naked men from Cnossos, smiling the archaic smile
of those that will without fail come back again,
and kindling little fires upon the shores
and crouching, and speaking the music of lost languages.

And the Minoan Gods, and the Gods of Tiryns
are heard softly laughing and chatting, as ever;
and Dionysos, young and a stranger
leans listening on the gate, in all respect.

FOR THE HEROES ARE DIPPED IN SCARLET

BEFORE Plato told the great lie of ideals
men slimly went like fishes, and didn't care.

They had long hair, like Samson,
and clean as arrows they sped at the mark
when the bow-cord twanged.

They knew it was no use knowing
their own nothingness:
for they were not nothing.

So now they come back! Hark!
Hark! the low and shattering laughter of bearded men
with the slim waists of warriors, and the long feet
of moon-lit dancers.

Oh, and their faces scarlet, like the dolphin's blood!
Lo! the loveliest is red all over, rippling vermilion
as he ripples upwards!
laughing in his black beard!

They are dancing! they return, as they went, dancing!
For the thing that is done without the glowing as of god,
        vermilion,
were best not done at all.
How glistening red they are!

DEMIURGE

THEY say that reality exists only in the spirit
that corporal existence is a kind of death
that pure being is bodiless
that the idea of the form precedes the form substantial.

But what nonsense it is!
as if any Mind could have imagined a lobster
dozing in the under-deeps, then reaching out a savage and iron
        claw!

Even the mind of God can only imagine
those things that have become themselves:
bodies and presences, here and now, creatures with a foothold
        in creation
even if it is only a lobster on tip-toe.

Religion knows better than philosophy.
Religion knows that Jesus was never Jesus
till he was born from a womb, and ate soup and bread
and grew up, and became, in the wonder of creation, Jesus,
with a body and with needs, and a lovely spirit.

RED GERANIUM AND GODLY MIGNONETTE

IMAGINE that any mind ever *thought* a red geranium!
As if the redness of a red geranium could be anything but a
    sensual experience
and as if sensual experience could take place before there were
    any senses.
We know that even God could not imagine the redness of a red
    geranium
nor the smell of mignonette
when geraniums were not, and mignonette neither.
And even when they were, even God would have to have a
    nose to smell at the mignonette.
You can't imagine the Holy Ghost sniffing at cherry-pie
    heliotrope.
Or the Most High, during the coal age, cudgelling his mighty
    brains
even if he had any brains: straining his mighty mind
to think, among the moss and mud of lizards and mastodons
to think out, in the abstract, when all was twilit green and
    muddy:
'Now there shall be tum-tiddly-um, and tum-tiddly-um,
hey-presto! scarlet geranium!'
We know it couldn't be done.

But imagine, among the mud and the mastodons
God sighing and yearning with tremendous creative yearning,
    in that dark green mess
oh, for some other beauty, some other beauty
that blossomed at last, red geranium, and mignonette.

THE BODY OF GOD

GOD is the great urge that has not yet found a body
but urges towards incarnation with the great creative urge.

And becomes at last a clove carnation: lo! that is god!
and becomes at last Helen, or Ninon: any lovely and generous
    woman
at her best and her most beautiful, being god, made manifest,
any clear and fearless man being god, very god.

There is no god
apart from poppies and the flying fish,
men singing songs, and women brushing their hair in the sun.
The lovely things are god that has come to pass, like Jesus
    came.
The rest, the undiscoverable, is the demi-urge.

THE RAINBOW

EVEN the rainbow has a body
made of the drizzling rain
and is an architecture of glistening atoms
built up, built up
yet you can't lay your hand on it,
nay, nor even your mind.

THE MAN OF TYRE

THE man of Tyre went down to the sea
pondering, for he was Greek, that God is one and all alone and
    ever more shall be so.
And a woman who had been washing clothes in the pool of
    rock
where a stream came down to the gravel of the sea and sank in,

who had spread white washing on the gravel banked above the
    bay,
who had lain her shift on the shore, on the shingle slope,
who had waded to the pale green sea of evening, out to a shoal,
pouring sea-water over herself
now turned, and came slowly back, with her back to the
    evening sky.

Oh lovely, lovely with the dark hair piled up, as she went
    deeper, deeper down the channel, then rose shallower,
    shallower,
with the full thighs slowly lifting of the wader wading
    shorewards
and the shoulders pallid with light from the silent sky behind
both breasts dim and mysterious, with the glamorous kindness
    of twilight between them
and the dim blotch of black maidenhair like an indicator,
giving a message to the man —

So in the cane-brake he clasped his hands in delight
that could only be god-given, and murmured:
Lo! God is one god! But here in the twilight
godly and lovely comes Aphrodite out of the sea
towards me!

THEY SAY THE SEA IS LOVELESS

THEY say the sea is loveless, that in the sea
love cannot live, but only bare, salt splinters
of loveless life.
But from the sea
the dolphins leap round Dionysos' ship
whose masts have purple vines,
and up they come with the purple dark of rainbows
and flip! they go! with the nose-dive of sheer delight:
and the sea is making love to Dionysos
in the bouncing of these small and happy whales.

WHALES WEEP NOT!

THEY say the sea is cold, but the sea contains
the hottest blood of all, and the wildest, the most urgent.

All the whales in the wider deeps, hot are they, as they urge
on and on, and dive beneath the icebergs.
The right whales, the sperm-whales, the hammer-heads, the
    killers
there they blow, there they blow, hot wild white breath out of
    the sea!

And they rock, and they rock, through the sensual ageless ages
on the depths of the seven seas,
and through the salt they reel with drunk delight
and in the tropics tremble they with love
and roll with massive, strong desire, like gods.
Then the great bull lies up against his bride
in the blue deep bed of the sea,
as mountain pressing on mountain, in the zest of life:
and out of the inward roaring of the inner red ocean of
    whale-blood
the long tip reaches strong, intense, like the maelstrom-tip, and
    comes to rest
in the clasp and the soft, wild clutch of a she-whale's
    fathomless body.

And over the bridge of the whale's strong phallus, linking the
    wonder of whales
the burning archangels under the sea keep passing, back and
    forth,
keep passing, archangels of bliss
from him to her, from her to him, great Cherubim
that wait on whales in mid-ocean, suspended in the waves of
    the sea
great heaven of whales in the waters, old hierarchies.

And enormous mother whales lie dreaming suckling their
    whale-tender young
and dreaming with strange whale eyes wide open in the waters
    of the beginning and the end.

And bull-whales gather their women and whale-calves in a
    ring
when danger threatens, on the surface of the ceaseless flood
and range themselves like great fierce Seraphim facing the
    threat
encircling their huddled monsters of love.
And all this happens in the sea, in the salt
where God is also love, but without words:
and Aphrodite is the wife of whales
most happy, happy she!

and Venus among the fishes skips and is a she-dolphin
she is the gay, delighted porpoise sporting with love and the
    sea
she is the female tunny-fish, round and happy among the males
and dense with happy blood, dark rainbow bliss in the sea.

INVOCATION TO THE MOON

You beauty, O you beauty
you glistening garmentless beauty!
great lady, great glorious lady
greatest of ladies
crownless and jewelless and garmentless
because naked you are more wonderful than anything we can
    stroke —

Be good to me, lady, great lady of the nearest
heavenly mansion, and last!
Now I am at your gate, you beauty, you lady of all nakedness!
Now I must enter your mansion, and beg your gift
Moon, O Moon, great lady of the heavenly few.

Far and forgotten is the Villa of Venus the glowing
and behind me now in the gulfs of space lies the golden house
    of the sun,
and six have given me gifts, and kissed me god-speed
kisses of four great lords, beautiful, as they held me to their
    bosom in farewell
and kiss of the far-off lingering lady who looks over the distant
    fence of the twilight,
and one warm kind kiss of the lion with golden paws —

Now, lady of the Moon, now open the gate of your silvery
    house
and let me come past the silver bells of your flowers, and the
    cockle-shells
into your house, garmentless lady of the last great gift:
who will give me back my lost limbs
and my lost white fearless breast
and set me again on moon-remembering feet
a healed, whole man, O Moon!

Lady, lady of the last house down the long, long street of the
    stars
be good to me now, as I beg you, as you've always been good
    to men
who begged of you and gave you homage
and watched for your glistening feet down the garden path!

BUTTERFLY

Butterfly, the wind blows sea-ward, strong beyond the
    garden wall!
Butterfly, why do you settle on my shoe, and sip the dirt on my
    shoe,
lifting your veined wings, lifting them? big white butterfly!

Already it is October, and the wind blows strong to the sea
from the hills where snow must have fallen, the wind is
    polished with snow.
Here in the garden, with red geraniums, it is warm, it is warm
but the wind blows strong to sea-ward, white butterfly,
    content on my shoe!

Will you go, will you go from my warm house?
Will you climb on your big soft wings, black-dotted,
as up an invisible rainbow, an arch
till the wind slides you sheer from the arch-crest
and in a strange level fluttering you go out to sea-ward, white
    speck!

Farewell, farewell, lost soul!
you have melted in the crystalline distance,
it is enough! I saw you vanish into air.

BAVARIAN GENTIANS

NOT every man has gentians in his house
in soft September, at slow, sad Michaelmas.

Bavarian gentians, tall and dark, but dark
darkening the daytime torch-like with the smoking blueness of
    Pluto's gloom,
ribbed hellish flowers erect, with their blaze of darkness spread
    blue,
blown flat into points, by the heavy white draught of the day.

Torch-flowers of the blue-smoking darkness, Pluto's dark-blue
    blaze
black lamps from the halls of Dis, smoking dark blue
giving off darkness, blue darkness, upon Demeter's
    yellow-pale day
Whom have you come for, here in the white-cast day?

Reach me a gentian, give me a torch!
let me guide myself with the blue, forked torch of a flower
down the darker and darker stairs, where blue is darkened on
      blueness
down the way Persephone goes, just now, in first-frosted
      September
to the sightless realm where darkness is married to dark
and Persephone herself is but a voice, as a bride
a gloom invisible enfolded in the deeper dark
of the arms of Pluto as he ravishes her once again
and pierces her once more with his passion of the utter dark
among the splendour of black-blue torches, shedding
      fathomless darkness on the nuptials.

Give me a flower on a tall stem, and three dark flames,
for I will go to the wedding, and be wedding-guest
at the marriage of the living dark.

LUCIFER

ANGELS are bright still, though the brightest fell.
But tell me, tell me, how do you know
he lost any of his brightness in the falling?
In the dark-blue depths, under layers and layers of darkness,
I see him move like the ruby, a gleam from within
of his own magnificence,
coming like the ruby in the invisible dark, glowing
with his own annunciation, towards us.

PAX

ALL that matters is to be at one with the living God
to be a creature in the house of the God of Life.

Like a cat asleep on a chair
at peace, in peace
and at one with the master of the house, with the mistress,

at home, at home in the house of the living,
sleeping on the hearth, and yawning before the fire.

Sleeping on the hearth of the living world
yawning at home before the fire of life
feeling the presence of the living God
like a great reassurance
a deep calm in the heart
a presence
as of the master sitting at the board
in his own and greater being,
in the house of life.

ONLY MAN

ONLY man can fall from God
Only man.

No animal, no beast nor creeping thing
no cobra nor hyaena nor scorpion nor hideous white ant
can slip entirely through the fingers of the hands of god
into the abyss of self-knowledge,
knowledge of the self-apart-from-god.

For the knowledge of the self-apart-from-God
is an abyss down which the soul can slip
writhing and twisting in all the revolutions
of the unfinished plunge
of self-awareness, now apart from God, falling
fathomless, fathomless, self-consciousness wriggling
writhing deeper and deeper in all the minutiae of
    self-knowledge, downwards, exhaustive,
yet never, never coming to the bottom, for there is no bottom;
zigzagging down like the fizzle from a finished rocket
the frizzling falling fire that cannot go out, dropping wearily,
neither can it reach the depth
for the depth is bottomless,

so it wriggles its way even further down, further down
at last in sheer horror of not being able to leave off
knowing itself, knowing itself apart from God, falling.

IN THE CITIES

In the cities
there is even no more any weather
the weather in town is always benzine, or else petrol fumes
lubricating oil, exhaust gas.

As over some dense marsh, the fumes
thicken, miasma, the fumes of the automobile
densely thicken in the cities.

In ancient Rome, down the thronged streets
no wheels might run, no insolent chariots.
Only the footsteps, footsteps
of people
and the gentle trotting of the litter-bearers.

In Minos, in Mycenae
in all the cities with lion gates
the dead threaded the air, lingering
lingering in the earth's shadow
and leaning towards the old hearth.

In London, New York, Paris
in the bursten cities
the dead tread heavily through the muddy air
through the mire of fumes
heavily, stepping weary on our hearts.

LORD'S PRAYER

FOR thine is the kingdom
the power, and the glory —

Hallowed be thy name, then
Thou who art nameless —

Give me, Oh give me
besides my daily bread
my kingdom, my power, and my glory.

All things that turn to thee
have their kingdom, their power, and their glory.

Like the kingdom of the nightingale at twilight
whose power and glory I have often heard and felt.

Like the kingdom of the fox in the dark
yapping in his power and his glory
which is death to the goose.

Like the power and the glory of the goose in the mist
honking over the lake.

And I, a naked man, calling
calling to thee for my mana,
my kingdom, my power, and my glory.

MANA OF THE SEA

DO you see the sea, breaking itself to bits against the islands
yet remaining unbroken, the level great sea?

Have I caught from it
the tide in my arms
that runs down to the shallows of my wrists, and breaks
abroad in my hands, like waves among the rocks of substance?

Do the rollers of the sea
roll down my thighs
and over the submerged islets of my knees
with power, sea-power
sea-power
to break against the ground
in the flat, recurrent breakers of my two feet?

And is my body ocean, ocean
whose power runs to the shores along my arms
and breaks in the foamy hands, whose power rolls out
to the white-treading waves of two salt feet?

I am the sea, I am the sea!

ANAXAGORAS

WHEN Anaxagoras says: Even snow is black!
he is taken by the scientists very seriously
because he is enunciating a 'principle', a 'law'
that all things are mixed, and therefore the purest white snow
has in it an element of blackness.

That they call science, and reality.
I call it mental conceit and mystification
and nonsense, for pure snow is white to us
white and white and only white
with a lovely bloom of whiteness upon white
in which the soul delights and the senses
have an experience of bliss.

And life is for delight, and for bliss
and dread, and the dark, rolling ominousness of doom.
Then the bright dawning of delight again
from off the sheer white snow, or the poised moon.

And in the shadow of the sun the snow is blue, so blue-aloof
with a hint of the frozen bells of the scylla flower
but never the ghost of a glimpse of Anaxagoras' funeral black.

KISSING AND HORRID STRIFE

I HAVE been defeated and dragged down by pain
and worsted by the evil world-soul of today.

But still I know that life is for delight
and for bliss
as now when the tiny wavelets of the sea
tip the morning light on edge, and spill it with delight
to show how inexhaustible it is.

And life is for delight, and bliss
like now when the white sun kisses the sea
and plays with the wavelets like a panther playing with its cubs
cuffing them with soft paws,
and blows that are caresses,
kisses of the soft-balled paws, where the talons are.

And life is for dread,
for doom that darkens, and the Sunderers
that sunder us from each other,
that strip us and destroy us and break us down
as the tall foxgloves and the mulleins and mallows
are torn down by dismembering autumn
till not a vestige is left, and black winter has no trace
of any such flowers;
and yet the roots below the blackness are intact:
the Thunderers and the Sunderers have their term,
their limit, their thus far and no further.

Life is for kissing and for horrid strife.
Life is for the angels and the Sunderers,
Life is for the daimons and the demons,

those that put honey on our lips, and those that put salt.
But life is not
for the dead vanity of knowing better, nor the blank
cold comfort of superiority, nor silly
conceit of being immune,
nor puerility of contradictions
like saying snow is black, or desire is evil.

Life is for kissing and for horrid strife,
the angels and the Sunderers.
And perhaps in unknown Death we perhaps shall know
Oneness and poised immunity.
But why then should we die while we can live?
And while we live
the kissing and communing cannot cease
nor yet the striving and the horrid strife.

WHEN SATAN FELL

WHEN Satan fell, he only fell
because the Lord Almighty rose a bit too high,
a bit beyond himself.

So Satan only fell to keep a balance.
'Are you so lofty, O my God?
Are you so pure and lofty, up aloft?
Then I will fall, and plant the paths to hell
with vines and poppies and fig-trees
so that lost souls may eat grapes
and the moist fig
and put scarlet buds in their hair on the way to hell,
on the way to dark perdition.'

And hell and heaven are the scales of the balance of life
which swing against each other.

DEATH IS NOT EVIL, EVIL IS MECHANICAL

ONLY the human being, absolved from kissing and strife
goes on and on and on, without wandering
fixed upon the hub of the ego
going, yet never wandering, fixed, yet in motion,
the kind of hell that is real, grey and awful
sinless and stainless going round and round
the kind of hell grey Dante never saw
but of which he had a bit inside him.

Know thyself, and that thou art mortal.
But know thyself, denying that thou art mortal:
a thing of kisses and strife
a lit-up shaft of rain
a calling column of blood
a rose tree bronzey with thorns
a mixture of yea and nay
a rainbow of love and hate
a wind that blows back and forth
a creature of beautiful peace, like a river
and a creature of conflict, like a cataract:
know thyself, in denial of all these things —

And thou shalt begin to spin round on the hub of the obscene
    ego
a grey void thing that goes without wandering
a machine that in itself is nothing
a centre of the evil world-soul.

THE SHIP OF DEATH

HAVE you built your ship of death, oh have you?
Oh build your ship of death, for you will need it.

Now in the twilight, sit by the invisible sea
Of peace, and build your little ship
Of death, that will carry the soul
On its last journey, on and on, so still
So beautiful, over the last of seas.

When the day comes, that will come.
Oh think of it in the twilight peacefully!
The last day, and the setting forth
On the longest journey, over the hidden sea
To the last wonder of oblivion.

Oblivion, the last wonder!
When we have trusted ourselves entirely
To the unknown, and are taken up
Out of our little ships of death
Into pure oblivion.

Oh build your ship of death, be building it now
With dim, calm thoughts and quiet hands
Putting its timbers together in the dusk,

Rigging its mast with the silent, invisible sail
That will spread in death to the breeze
Of the kindness of the cosmos, that will waft
The little ship with its soul to the wonder-goal.

Ah, if you want to live in peace on the face of the earth
Then build your ship of death, in readiness
For the longest journey, over the last of seas.

TABERNACLE

COME, let us build a temple to oblivion
with seven veils, and an innermost
Holy of Holies of sheer oblivion.

And there oblivion dwells, and the silent soul
may sink into god at last, having passed the veils.

But anyone who shall ascribe attributes to God or oblivion
let him be cast out, for blasphemy.
For God is a deeper forgetting far than sleep
and all description is a blasphemy.

SHADOWS

AND if tonight my soul may find her peace
in sleep, and sink in good oblivion,
and in the morning wake like a new-opened flower
then I have been dipped again in God, and new-created.

And if, as weeks go round, in the dark of the moon
my spirit darkens and goes out, and soft, strange gloom
pervades my movements and my thoughts and words
then I shall know that I am walking still
with God, we are close together now the moon's in shadow.

And if, as autumn deepens and darkens
I feel the pain of falling leaves, and stems that break in storms
and trouble and dissolution and distress
and then the softness of deep shadows folding, folding
around my soul and spirit, around my lips
so sweet, like a swoon, or more like the drowse of a low, sad
    song
singing darker than the nightingale, on, on to the solstice
and the silence of short days, the silence of the year, the
    shadow,

then I shall know that my life is moving still
with the dark earth, and drenched
with the deep oblivion of earth's lapse and renewal.

And if, in the changing phases of man's life
I fall in sickness and in misery
my wrists seem broken and my heart seems dead
and strength is gone, and my life
is only the leavings of a life:

and still, among it all, snatches of lovely oblivion, and snatches
    of renewal
odd, wintry flowers upon the withered stem, yet new strange
    flowers
such as my life has not brought forth before, new blossoms of
    me —

then I must know that still
I am in the hands of the unknown God,
he is breaking me down to his own oblivion
to send me forth on a new morning, a new man.

APPENDIX

The text of 'The Ship of Death' used above is probably Lawrence's final version. He recoiled from too much probing of the mystery of death for reasons set out in 'Tabernacle'. The more familiar longer version is given here, together with the penultimate version of 'Bavarian Gentians' which, due to an error in Richard Aldington's editing of *Last Poems*, was for many years the received text.

BAVARIAN GENTIANS

NOT every man has gentians in his house
in soft September, at slow, sad Michaelmas.

Bavarian gentians, big and dark, only dark
darkening the day-time, torch-like, with the smoking blueness
    of Pluto's gloom,
ribbed and torch-like, with their blaze of darkness spread blue
down flattening into points, flattened under the sweep of white
    day
torch-flower of the blue-smoking darkness, Pluto's dark-blue
    daze,
black lamps from the halls of Dis, burning dark blue,
giving off darkness, blue darkness, as Demeter's pale lamps
    give off light,
lead me then, lead the way.

Reach me a gentian, give me a torch!
let me guide myself with the blue, forked torch of this flower

down the darker and darker stairs, where blue is darkened on
    blueness
even where Persephone goes, just now, from the frosted
    September
to the sightless realm where darkness is awake upon the dark
and Persephone herself is but a voice
or a darkness invisible enfolded in the deeper dark
of the arms Plutonic, and pierced with the passion of dense
    gloom,
among the splendour of torches of darkness, shedding
    darkness on the lost bride and her groom.

THE SHIP OF DEATH

I

Now it is autumn and the falling fruit
and the long journey towards oblivion.

The apples falling like great drops of dew
to bruise themselves an exit from themselves.

And it is time to go, to bid farewell
to one's own self, and find an exit
from the fallen self.

2

Have you built your ship of death, O have you?
O build your ship of death, for you will need it.

The grim frost is at hand, when the apples will fall
thick, almost thundrous, on the hardened earth.

And death is on the air like a smell of ashes!
Ah! can't you smell it?

And in the bruised body, the frightened soul
finds itself shrinking, wincing from the cold
that blows upon it through the orifices.

3

And can a man his own quietus make
with a bare bodkin?

With daggers, bodkins, bullets, man can make
a bruise or break of exit for his life;
but is that a quietus, O tell me, is it quietus?

Surely not so! for how could murder, even self-murder
ever a quietus make?

4

O let us talk of quiet that we know,
that we can know, the deep and lovely quiet
of a strong heart at peace!

How can we this, our own quietus, make?

5

Build then the ship of death, for you must take
the longest journey, to oblivion.

And die the death, the long and painful death
that lies between the old self and the new.

Already our bodies are fallen, bruised, badly bruised,
already our souls are oozing through the exit
of the cruel bruise.

Already the dark and endless ocean of the end
is washing in through the breaches of our wounds,
already the flood is upon us.

Oh build your ship of death, your little ark
and furnish it with food, with little cakes, and wine
for the dark flight down oblivion.

6

Piecemeal the body dies, and the timid soul
has her footing washed away, as the dark flood rises.

We are dying, we are dying, we are all of us dying
and nothing will stay the death-flood rising within us
and soon it will rise on the world, on the outside world.

We are dying, we are dying, piecemeal our bodies are dying
and our strength leaves us,
and our soul cowers naked in the dark rain over the flood,
cowering in the last branches of the tree of our life.

7

We are dying, we are dying, so all we can do
is now to be willing to die, and to build the ship
of death to carry the soul on the longest journey.

A little ship, with oars and food
and little dishes, and all accoutrements
fitting and ready for the departing soul.

Now launch the small ship, now as the body dies
and life departs, launch out, the fragile soul
in the fragile ship of courage, the ark of faith
with its store of food and little cooking pans
and change of clothes,

upon the flood's black waste
upon the waters of the end
upon the sea of death, where still we sail
darkly, for we cannot steer, and have no port.

There is no port, there is nowhere to go
only the deepening blackness darkening still
blacker upon the soundless, ungurgling flood
darkness at one with darkness, up and down
and sideways utterly dark, so there is no direction any more.
And the little ship is there; yet she is gone.
She is not seen, for there is nothing to see her by.
She is gone! gone! and yet
somewhere she is there.
Nowhere!

8

And everything is gone, the body is gone
completely under, gone, entirely gone.
The upper darkness is heavy as the lower,
between them the little ship
is gone
she is gone.

It is the end, it is oblivion.

9

And yet out of eternity, a thread
separates itself on the blackness,
a horizontal thread
that fumes a little with pallor upon the dark.

Is it illusion? or does the pallor fume
A little higher?
Ah wait, wait, for there's the dawn,
the cruel dawn of coming back to life
out of oblivion.

Wait, wait, the little ship
drifting, beneath the deathly ashy grey
of a flood-dawn.

Wait, wait! even so, a flush of yellow
and strangely, O chilled wan soul, a flush of rose.

A flush of rose, and the whole thing starts again.

10

The flood subsides, and the body, like a worn sea-shell
emerges strange and lovely.
And the little ship wings home, faltering and lapsing
on the pink flood,
and the frail soul steps out, into her house again
filling the heart with peace.

Swings the heart renewed with peace
even of oblivion.

Oh build your ship of death, oh build it!
for you will need it.
For the voyage of oblivion awaits you.

INDEX OF FIRST LINES

263

INDEX OF TITLES

FOR THE BEST IN PAPERBACKS, LOOK FOR THE

In every corner of the world, on every subject under the sun, Penguin represents quality and variety – the very best in publishing today.

For complete information about books available from Penguin – including Pelicans, Puffins, Peregrines and Penguin Classics – and how to order them, write to us at the appropriate address below. Please note that for copyright reasons the selection of books varies from country to country.

In the United Kingdom: Please write to *Dept E.P., Penguin Books Ltd, Harmondsworth, Middlesex, UB7 0DA*

In the United States: Please write to *Dept BA, Penguin, 299 Murray Hill Parkway, East Rutherford, New Jersey 07073*

In Canada: Please write to *Penguin Books Canada Ltd, 2801 John Street, Markham, Ontario L3R 1B4*

In Australia: Please write to the *Marketing Department, Penguin Books Australia Ltd, P.O. Box 257, Ringwood, Victoria 3134*

In New Zealand: Please write to the *Marketing Department, Penguin Books (NZ) Ltd, Private Bag, Takapuna, Auckland 9*

In India: Please write to *Penguin Overseas Ltd, 706 Eros Apartments, 56 Nehru Place, New Delhi, 110019*

In Holland: Please write to *Penguin Books Nederland B.V., Postbus 195, NL–1380AD Weesp, Netherlands*

In Germany: Please write to *Penguin Books Ltd, Friedrichstrasse 10–12, D–6000 Frankfurt Main 1, Federal Republic of Germany*

In Spain: Please write to *Longman Penguin España, Calle San Nicolas 15, E–28013 Madrid, Spain*

In France: Please write to *Penguin Books Ltd, 39 Rue de Montmorency, F-75003, Paris, France*

In Japan: Please write to *Longman Penguin Japan Co Ltd, Yamaguchi Building, 2–12–9 Kanda Jimbocho, Chiyoda-Ku, Tokyo 101, Japan*